If the Fa...

She'll live h...

In these contemporary twists on classic fairy tales from Harlequin Romance, allow yourself to be swept away on a jet-set adventure where the modern-day heroine is the star of the story. The journey toward happy-ever-after may not be easy, but in a land far away, true love will *always* result in their dreams coming true—especially with a little help from Prince Charming!

Get lost in the magic of...

Their Fairy Tale India Escape
by Ruby Basu

Part of His Royal World
by Nina Singh

Cinderella's Billion-Dollar Invitation
by Michele Renae

Beauty and the Playboy Prince
by Justine Lewis

All available now!

Dear Reader,

Thank you for picking up (or clicking on) *Beauty and the Playboy Prince* and embarking on a little fairy-tale escapism.

We often use the term "fairy tale" as synonymous with a happy ending, but traditional fairy tales often had darker sides (the Brothers Grimm, Hans Christian Andersen, I'm looking at you). Bad things often happened, especially to women and children, and the stories were later sanitized to resemble the ones we are familiar with today.

Being a royal these days is a little like a fairy tale— in all senses of the word. There might be castles and luxury, but there is also a darker side. Royals enjoy extreme privilege, but it often comes at a high price. Your life and privacy are no longer your own.

Royal status is my hero Ed's burden and destiny, but he is happy and willing to serve. His best friend, Simone, has experienced the darker side of royalty and fame and it isn't a path she wants to choose for herself. Instead, she is happy living above her secondhand bookshop in Paris, away from the public eye. But fate has other ideas for Ed and Simone. I won't give more away. I hope you enjoy their story.

Happy reading,

Justine

Beauty and the Playboy Prince

Justine Lewis

HARLEQUIN

Romance

Recycling programs
for this product may
not exist in your area.

ISBN-13: 978-1-335-59657-4

Beauty and the Playboy Prince

Copyright © 2024 by Justine Lewis

For questions and comments about the quality of this book, please contact us at CustomerService@Harlequin.com.

Harlequin Enterprises ULC
22 Adelaide St. West, 41st Floor
Toronto, Ontario M5H 4E3, Canada
www.Harlequin.com

Printed in U.S.A.

Justine Lewis writes uplifting, heartwarming contemporary romances. She lives in Australia with her hero husband, two teenagers and an outgoing puppy. When she isn't writing, she loves to walk her dog in the bush near her house, attempt to keep her garden alive and search for the perfect frock. She loves hearing from readers, and you can visit her at justinelewis.com.

Books by Justine Lewis

Harlequin Romance

Billionaire's Snowbound Marriage Reunion
Fiji Escape with Her Boss
Back in the Greek Tycoon's World

Visit the Author Profile page
at Harlequin.com.

For Robby and serendipitous meetings.

Praise for
Justine Lewis

"Justine Lewis will capture every reader's heart with her poignant, intense and dramatic contemporary romance, *Billionaire's Snowbound Marriage Reunion*. A beautifully written tale...this affecting romantic read will move readers to tears and have them falling in love with both Lily and Jack."

—*Goodreads*

PROLOGUE

The Cursed Kingdom
Florenan Fairy Tales, 1786

ONCE UPON A time there was a beautiful kingdom, high in the Alps. In the summer the valleys were green and lush. In the winter snow capped the beautiful peaks. Perched in that kingdom was a beautiful palace and in that palace lived a king.

But the King took all his subjects' money and spent it on cards, dice and horses. His wife left him, taking all the crown jewels. The kingdom was almost bankrupt.

A witch placed a curse over the kingdom saying that the kingdom would be destroyed if the King's sons followed their father and put their own base desires before their people. The witch prophesied that the kingdom could only be saved by a prince who was brave and true and who put his family and his people above himself.

The first Prince loved wine so much he ignored his wife and neglected his country. His wife died of loneliness and a giant earthquake shook the country nearly causing it to crumble into ruins.

The second Prince thought that he had evaded detection by the witch and her curse. He secretly loved many women who were not his wife until one day when he became so distracted by his lovers that the kingdom was invaded. The war ripped the country apart and the Prince had to flee.

And the third Prince? The third Prince vowed to break the curse by always putting his duty first. By staying true to his country and not his base desires.

The third Prince vowed never to marry.

CHAPTER ONE

SIMONE SAID *AU REVOIR* to her last customer, closed the door to the bookshop and slid the steel lock across with a satisfying clunk. In the small office behind the counter, she turned on the television to check on the tennis scores and got to work reconciling the day's accounts. She needed to be quick if she was going to meet her friends, Julia and André, at the bistro down the street.

Tallying the days' takings was thankfully taking longer these days. Business had been steadily picking up over the past few months and she was back on track working towards her savings goal to enable her to, hopefully, buy the bookshop within the next few years.

The bookshop, The Last Chapter, was situated in Simone's favourite part of Paris, the Latin Quarter. Also known as the Fifth Arrondissement, the Latin Quarter was characterised by the sound of bells from churches small and large, the thick wooden doors hiding secret courtyards and the narrow laneways, all winding their way up the gentle hill to the Pantheon.

It was home to black ironwork decorating the windows, flower boxes with blooms of all colours. At street level, it was home to the tempting boulangeries, patisseries, fromageries and wine shops selling world-class wines that even students could afford.

This was a place of students, intellectuals, readers, dreamers with hundreds of years of learning. And, when you were particularly lucky, the smell of baking croissants.

Simone didn't even mind the tourists. They came from all over the world, bringing their own experiences, thoughts and dreams to Paris as they had been doing for centuries. Besides, tourists made up half of her customers.

Simone's boss was a British investor named Mr Grant. He owned the building and the business and spoke regularly about closing the bookshop and opening a convenience store instead. Simone had worked in the bookshop for nearly eight years and had managed it for five. She also lived in a studio apartment on the sixth floor of the same building.

'The bookshop is over a hundred years old,' she'd reminded Mr Grant. 'Think of all the history!'

It was the history of The Last Chapter that had convinced Mr Grant to keep the business operating for a while longer, while Simone saved enough money to be able to purchase it from him.

She glanced at the small television, looking for the tennis scores, but the headline on the ticker tape across the bottom of the screen made her suck in a sharp breath. *Mon Dieu.*

A woman was claiming to be pregnant with the King of Florena's child. The claim might have made some people express shock, but most would simply shrug. If Florena had been any other small European kingdom Simone probably would have done the same. However, Simone had spent the first sixteen years of her life not only in Florena, but in the royal residence, Castle Villeneuve, itself. She knew the King and his family. While she didn't return to Florena often, it was still her home. Her mother still lived there, working for the royal family. Simone could only imagine what they must all be going through.

King Edouard and Queen Isabella had always given the appearance of being, if not a happy couple, at least a functioning one. Their union had resulted in just one child, Prince Edouard, known to Simone as Ed, born exactly nine months after their wedding.

The marriage hadn't been arranged, but it had been beneficial to both. Isabella was the daughter and sole heir of one of the richest men in the world. The royal family of Florena had been struggling financially and reputationally after King Edouard's father, Old King Edouard, had wasted the royal family's private fortune with his reckless spending and womanising. Queen Isabella's fortune had meant the royals did not have to seek assistance from Florenan taxpayers, which had settled the republican cries from certain politicians.

Isabella gained a title and status, the country benefited from the money and connections she brought with her, and the kingdom gained peace and stability.

Young and good-looking, the King and Queen had probably hoped that love would grow.

It hadn't.

But this hadn't been merely indifference. The King had been having an affair and had fathered a child that wasn't the Queen's. Simone's thoughts went to the Queen, but her heart went out to Ed. Her childhood friend and companion.

She grabbed her phone to search for more information than the television was offering her. A twenty-six-year-old woman, Celine, claimed to be in a two-year relationship with King Edouard, who was thirty years her senior. She was now pregnant with their child. The King, or indeed any member of the royal family, was yet to comment. The Queen was reportedly in the Caribbean. The King was in Florena, but hadn't left the palace. And the Prince?

No one knew.

His last official engagement had been in New York as part of his duties as the Florenan trade envoy to North America. Ed's position as trade envoy might have seemed nepotistic, until you learnt that he spoke five languages and held degrees in economics and international relations. Few other thirty-year-olds were as qualified as he was to represent his country.

There was a knock at the door and she groaned. The *Closed* sign, written in seven languages, no less, was clearly visible. She contemplated pretending she wasn't there, but the customer knocked again, hard enough that she worried about the old glass pane shattering.

She poked her head out of her office.

The customer was a taller than average male. He was wearing a baseball cap and, despite the unseasonably warm autumn day, a coat and scarf.

She could have let him in, a customer was a customer after all, but his insistent knocking made her pause.

'Simone, it's me. Let me in.'

Simone moved around the counter and to the door. The man cupped his hands around his face to block out the streetlight and pushed his nose against the old glass to look inside. Their eyes met and she stopped. Green eyes that could still, despite much wishing otherwise, make her heart stop.

It was really him.

Ed.

'Sim, please.'

What was he doing here now? Just when her life was going smoothly. When she was doing just great, thank you very much.

She slid the lock back, but before she turned the knob she paused, took a deep breath, and repeated the mantra she had perfected over the years.

Don't fall. Don't fall.

His palms were pressed against the glass and above them his green eyes pleaded. She pulled open the door and he fell inside, almost landing on her.

'Oh, Sim. Thank goodness.'

'Ed! What on earth are you doing here? Haven't you heard?'

'Why do you think I'm here?'

Ed pulled his cap off, revealing the same mass of light brown curls that had always topped his head, now cut short at the sides and slightly tamed. She wasn't sure how she felt about that.

It's not any of your business how handsome he looks or how he's chosen to wear his hair.

Simone locked the door behind him, still confused. Befuddled. Shocked. And no less clear about what was happening. Ed clearly wasn't in a hurry to enlighten her. He looked around the bookshop.

The Last Chapter was older than any of Simone's grandparents. It covered the ground and first storeys of a narrow slice of the street. Its two floors, along with a substantial part of the narrow staircases, were covered in second-hand books written in several different languages. The previous owner had liked to tell customers that F Scott Fitzgerald, Ernest Hemingway and Gertrude Stein had visited the bookshop—claims that Simone had long ago decided never to try to verify in case they proved false.

Ed put his hands on his hips and surveyed the small room as though he were surveying his vast estates.

'So this is the famous bookshop.'

'I don't think it's famous,' she replied.

She'd made The Last Chapter thrive since she'd

taken over the management, but it wasn't yet Shakespeare and Co.

'In the palace it is.'

Simone winced at the idea that they might talk about her at the palace.

'It's great to visit it at last.'

Implicit in his comment was that in the eight years she had managed the bookshop he had never bothered to drop in for a visit.

Though why would he? Even though they had grown up together they had seen very little of one another in the past decade, ever since she was sent away to school and banished from Florena.

'Ed, I don't understand. What's going on?'

'It's lovely. Cosy, rustic. And you've perfectly captured that ancient book aroma.' He picked up the closest book, an old copy of *Florenan Fairy Tales*, thumbed the pages and made a show of breathing in the scent.

An exasperated groan escaped her throat. 'Edouard. Please. What's going on?'

At the sound of his full name Ed's shoulders tensed.

Ed replaced the book from exactly where he had taken it, but still didn't speak.

He walked along the nearest shelf and ran his finger along it, as though searching for something. She didn't know what he was looking for, but doubted he would find it in her small section of German crime novels. He stopped and sighed, but still didn't turn.

Her heart swelled and broke at the same time. Ed was in her bookshop. His beautiful hands touching her books. His tall frame only just fitting under the low ceilings. He was in the same room as her, breathing in the same air, for the first time in years.

'You've heard?'

'Yes. Just then. On the news. But—'

'I expect everyone's heard.'

She might have seen the headline, but she had no idea what Celine's pregnancy would mean for Florena. The country was a small, progressive constitutional monarchy, but still. She had no idea how the royal family would navigate an illegitimate child. Apart from anything, the news must be personally devastating for the Queen. And for Ed.

'Ed, is it really true? It's really your father's child?'

A half-sibling for Ed.

'I assume so.' He shrugged. The attempt at nonchalance didn't hide the stress on his face, which in turn couldn't mask the heartbreak in his eyes.

'When did you…? I mean how long has it been going on?'

'A while.'

'You knew?'

'I knew he was seeing her, yes.'

She tried to keep her expression neutral, knew she'd failed. 'Your mother? Does she know?'

He laughed. 'Celine called her two days ago to tell her.'

'Oh.' Simone didn't even want to imagine how that phone call might have gone. 'But what does it mean? For your parents? For Florena? For Celine?' Simone was a little ashamed that Celine came as an afterthought. She didn't know her, but still.

'Who knows?' Ed threw his arms up to the low ceiling. 'That's what everyone at the palace is tearing their hair out about. If this had happened two hundred years ago Celine would've been given a house, a generous pension and the child would've been given a title. But now?'

Ed glanced out of the window. It was dark outside now and with the lights on any passer-by could see inside the bookshop.

'Is there somewhere more private we could go?' He nodded to the back room. 'I'm trying to keep a low profile.'

'Wait in my office for a moment and let me finish up. I'll be two minutes.'

Simone turned off the television and her computer, checked the alarm system and picked up her phone and keys.

She showed Ed through the storeroom and to the back door.

'It's very rambling, isn't it?' he said.

'I hope that's a compliment,' she grumbled.

'Of course. It's lovely.'

His attempt at flattery grated more than it should have because it highlighted the gulf between them.

He would inherit a palace that she had merely lived in as the child of a cook.

The back door led to a staircase that took them up the five flights of stairs to her attic.

'Is there an elevator?' he asked at around the third flight.

'Yes, but I thought you'd like to work on your figure.'

She knew he'd get the joke. Ed was in as good shape as ever. No one could miss his strong, lean legs, washboard stomach, and shoulders that could rival those of a champion rower.

She wasn't in bad shape herself. After all she walked up and down these stairs several times a day. She still felt self-conscious, though, with him walking behind her, unable to miss the sight of her legs and bottom ascending the stairs, even if he'd wanted to. Not that he had ever, in the twenty-five years they had known one another, shown the slightest interest in her physically.

Once they reached the sixth floor, she slid her keys into the lock and paused before pushing open the door. She shouldn't be ashamed. She loved her apartment. It was perfectly big enough for her and her cat, Belle, and she was proud to be managing her own business.

But she couldn't help looking at her apartment through Ed's eyes. It wasn't vast or stylish. It was most definitely quaint. Too bad. If Ed couldn't see its charm then he could just leave.

She pushed open the door to her one-room apartment.

He placed his small black backpack on her sofa and looked around. One half of the room was her living quarters, with a soft, cotton-covered sofa, a table just large enough for two chairs, some plants, bright prints on the walls and a small bookshelf—because you still needed books, even if you did have an entire bookshop downstairs.

In the other half of the room, behind a gauze curtain that psychologically separated the spaces, but didn't provide much actual privacy, was her double bed.

The kitchen was basic, with only a small fridge, a single sink, an oven and small bench space. Despite being raised by a chef, or maybe because of it, Simone didn't often cook. The bathroom was large enough to fit a sink, shower and toilet, but not much else.

'Is this all? Is there another room?'

She made sure her glare was withering. 'It's an attic in the Fifth Arrondissement and I manage a second-hand bookshop. I'm doing very well to afford this.'

'I meant, isn't it charming?' he said.

'Were you expecting Versailles?'

'No, Simone. It's lovely. Truly.' He sat on her small sofa, lay back and spread out his arms, making himself quite comfortable. She looked at him, at a loss of where to begin.

Once upon a time, as the fairy tale went, they had been close friends. Friends who squabbled, but adored one another at the same time. He was a year older than she and had been in her life for nearly as long as she could remember. Simone's father had died when she was only four and she and her mother, Alea, had been invited to move into one of the small apartments in the back of the palace, where Alea worked as a cook.

Ed was the only other child who lived in the palace and, even though Ed was the Prince, and she the daughter of one of the staff, the two children had found one another. When Ed hadn't been at school, or doing what young princes did, he'd always sought her out.

Simone had attended day school, and had certainly not done any of the aristocratic activities he had, like horse riding or skiing, so she'd always been around in the palace somewhere. In the kitchen with her mother, in the garden with the dogs, or riding her bike around the beautiful grounds.

The two of them had squabbled and teased each other, but they'd always had one another for company on the weekends when he was home from school and during some of the holidays.

Being with him now was familiar, almost like going home.

She told herself her feelings for him were only platonic, because of their long friendship. Because he reminded her of simpler times. Because he'd been with her through some of the saddest times of her childhood.

Not because the sight of him made her heart race. Or because catching a breath of his scent could make her head swoon. Or because she trembled just thinking about pressing her body up against his and…

Platonic. That was all her feelings were. All they ever would be. She might have had a childish crush on Ed once upon a time, but she had well and truly moved past that. She'd had to.

'Wine?' she asked.

'I thought you'd never ask.'

'It's not fancy.'

'Thank goodness. I plan to drink it quickly.'

She hid her smile. They would be fine. Two old friends catching up over a drink. She could manage this without getting any ideas that it might be something more. She took a bottle of cheap Bordeaux from the rack and uncorked it before sitting on the sofa next to him, being careful not to brush against him.

She poured two generous glasses and let him take a few sips before saying, 'I'm so sorry again. What a shock.'

He shrugged. 'Yes, but also no. The thing I can't get my head around is that I'm going to have a half-sibling. At thirty!'

Ed was at the age where he might have been having children himself, but he was the Playboy Prince. Unmarried. Unattached. And seemingly proud of it.

'Have you spoken to your mother? How is she?'

'Furious. He's always been much more discreet.'

'What do you mean? Always?'

'About all his affairs.'

'*All* his affairs? There've been others?'

Ed gave her another quizzical look. 'You must have known.'

'I mean… I guess I didn't think he'd been faithful. But two years is a relationship.'

'I mean, *you* must have known.' He stared at her, waiting for a response.

'I've never had an affair with him!'

He burst into laughter. 'That's not I meant.'

What did he mean? What did any of it mean?

'Ed, what's going on? Why are you here?'

He put his glass down. 'I was actually hoping I might be able to stay.'

CHAPTER TWO

'STAY? HERE?' Ed watched as Simone looked around her apartment, such as it was. If he'd realised she lived in a studio he might have thought twice. But his need to see Simone had overwhelmed everything else. When he'd received the phone call from his father, telling him he was going to have a baby brother or sister, one of his first thoughts had been of Simone. Growing up, she had always been there for him. And now he needed her more than ever.

Ed had jumped on the first plane from New York to Paris as soon as he'd received his father's order to come home. But in the seven hours it had taken the plane to cross the Atlantic further developments had caused his father to call again and say, 'Stay where you are. Lie low.'

When his father had said this, Ed had thought of Simone again and how fortunate it was that he had flown into Paris. She was safety, security and home.

His parents' marriage had always been unhappy. His home not filled with love, but with tension. From his early childhood Simone and her mother, Alea, had provided the home he craved. Even though they had drifted apart over the years, Simone was still the person he trusted most in the world. The news that he would have a sibling had made that suddenly very clear to him. He'd *needed* to see her.

He realised now he'd put his own selfish feelings

above any thought for her reality. The apartment, which was really just one room, was barely large enough for Simone. If she lived here with someone else then they must share a very intimate relationship. He looked at the bed, possibly the smallest double he'd ever seen. The idea of sharing a small bed with Simone sent an unexpected jolt through him. The tabloids might say that he, the Playboy Prince, was happy to share a bed with the nearest warm body, but the tabloids exaggerated. And Simone wasn't like any other woman. She was his oldest and dearest friend.

The sofa where they sat was on the same scale as the bed: cosy. He and Simone sat hip to hip on the sofa, which wasn't unpleasant, but the warmth of Simone's leg against his was certainly distracting. Two years it had been, maybe three, since they'd seen one another. And she was different, though he couldn't pinpoint why.

'I know it's sudden. Celine spoke publicly before the palace got their story straight and a plan in place. Press are camped outside the palace, with more flying into Florena each hour. Father told me to stay here and lie low. It'll probably just be one night.'

Simone drew and released a deep breath before saying, 'Yes, of course. But don't you need to be there?'

'You'd think,' he mumbled, mostly to himself.

While it would be years—decades, even—before

he became King, he was still the Prince. The King's only child. He wanted to be there to help. The matter involved him too. Most of all he wanted to help his father decide on the plan of action. The King had several options, but there was one in particular Ed really didn't want him to choose.

'Maybe he wants to spare you from it?'

'It's his scandal, not mine. Doesn't it look worse if I'm not there? Like I don't support him?'

'I don't know.'

She shrugged and looked as confused as he felt. In the craziness of the past day it was such a relief to be here, with her. She lifted her feet and tucked them under her bottom. He liked her hair. It was even longer than when he'd seen her last. Dark blonde, and falling in messy waves down her back. Her face was shaped like a heart and her eyes as brown and bright as ever.

She had been adorable as a kid, with big eyes, blonde curls and chubby cheeks. He wasn't quite used to her seeing her older. Grown up. He still sometimes saw the four-year-old he had unexpectedly stumbled across one day in his garden. He hadn't been much older. No one had told him another kid was moving in. Discovering her playing with his dog had been like magic. A friend he'd always wanted. A playmate who would play hide and seek and all sorts of games with him. A confidante who, despite their different backgrounds, still understood what it was like to live in the beautiful yet secluded palace.

He also remembered her as an uncertain teenager. The friend he'd seek out when he returned from school every holiday. Simone and Alea's apartment in the palace had been an oasis away from his cold parents. Alea's kitchen always warm and welcoming. His parents didn't even love each other enough to bicker, but Simone and her mother had always shown unconditional love and support. When someone mentioned the word 'home' his thoughts always flickered to Simone's apartment before duty focused them back on the palace proper.

Now, sitting on the sofa next to him, he saw child, teenager and woman all at once. The chubbiness of her cheeks had vanished, leaving cheekbones. Her bright blonde curls were darker and heavy with the weight of her thick, long hair. But her beautiful big brown round eyes remained the same. And they were looking at him now with concern.

'What do you think will happen? With your parents…?'

'Divorce? Probably. But then there's the issue of Mother's money. Her fortune has been paying for the running and the upkeep of the palaces and the family's expenses. Mother's father left me some money, but it is nowhere near the same amount. Besides, I don't know if she'll give Father the satisfaction of being able to marry Celine. It could get messy. I don't know if he even wants to marry Celine.'

'What about the baby?'

'I'm sure he'll look after it. He'll have to acknowledge it.'

A baby. A sibling. Twenty-four hours later he was still struggling to process the news. Ed couldn't think of another monarchy that had faced such a crisis in modern times. Sure, there were monarchs who had kids out of wedlock. But usually not when they were still married to someone else.

It would be a good enough reason, he thought, to get rid of the monarchy altogether.

The Florenans were generally proud of their independence, but there were always those who argued that the country would be better off if it were subsumed into another larger country. Like France or Italy. The current Prime Minister, Pierre Laurent, was in favour of making closer ties with France, the country of his birth. Ed had tried to raise his concerns about Laurent with his father, but the King had laughed them off.

'Nonsense. The people will never agree to that. I've seen off six Prime Ministers. Besides, the people love us. The House of Berringer has been around for five hundred years and we'll be here long after Pierre Laurent.'

Simone poured him another glass of wine and topped hers up. 'I don't have anything much to eat, I'm afraid. I could order something in.'

'Whatever you were going to have would be fine,' he said.

She looked down. 'I was going out.'

He was an idiot. He should have realised that she had a life. Plans.

'I'm sorry. A hot date?'

'No, just dinner with some friends.'

The relief he felt when she said that was almost physical, but he still said, 'You should go. I'll be fine here.'

How would he have felt if she had said she had a date? Uneasy? Sad? And that was silly. Simone was his friend.

She's probably had many boyfriends you don't know about. Look at her, she's gorgeous.

He was trying not to look at her, because each time he did his body tensed and his head became lighter.

Exhaustion. That was all it was. Nothing more. This was Simone, and he didn't get tense or light-headed around Simone.

'No. It's okay. I see them all the time. I haven't seen you in…'

Two years.

She'd seemed to avoid Florena more and more the older she got.

'You didn't visit last Christmas.'

'Managing the bookshop…it's too hard. I open every day, except Christmas.'

'You work seven days a week?'

She shrugged. 'I'm saving up to buy this place one day.'

'Really?'

'Yes.' She sat up straight. 'What's wrong with that?'

'Nothing, it's great. This apartment?'

She nodded. 'And the bookshop. And I'm on track.'

'Wow, that's great.'

'You sound surprised.'

He was, but that was on him, not her. They hadn't spent much time together at all in the past decade, and without him realising it she'd become a grown-up. Not just a grown-up. A successful, impressive, beautiful grown-up. Who was about to own a bookshop and an apartment in the middle of Paris. She'd flourished since leaving Florena as a sixteen-year-old.

'I'm impressed, but not surprised.'

She gave him a crooked grin. Even when she made a face she was gorgeous.

Something inside him twisted. She didn't have a hot date tonight but was there someone special around? If there was he wanted to meet him.

And yet he also didn't.

'So, is it just you living here?' That sounded casual enough.

'Oh, no. My five flatmates are out.'

He stared, open-mouthed, long enough for her to laugh.

'Of course it's just me. There's barely room enough for you!'

He felt his face warm. 'I meant, is there…? That is, are you seeing anyone?'

Now it was her time to pause and study his face before answering. It was none of his business if she was seeing someone, but as her friend he wanted to know. He needed to know that she was all right. That whoever she was with was not someone like his cheating father.

She tilted her head to one side, delaying her answer even longer. With every moment the pause lasted a knot grew tighter and tighter in his stomach.

She was seeing someone. And it was serious. She was about to tell him she was engaged. Or about to be.

And he realised he didn't want that. That was… wrong. Simone married to some Parisian.

'No. There's no one.'

He exhaled. More loudly than he'd expected. Why had she taken so long to answer? More to the point, why had so much seemed to hang on her answer?

He and Simone were only friends. Besides, Ed had no plans to enter into a serious relationship— now or ever. Royal marriages were rarely happy marriages. They had even less chance than celebrity matches. Edouard Henri Guillaume, Prince of Florena, was the latest in a long line of Princes Edouard, none of whom were known for their fidelity.

His father's scandal was just the latest in a long line. Ed was not going to risk his country's future on a royal marriage that would likely end the same way.

While Ed's faithfulness had never been tested—he'd never had a relationship that had lasted long enough to give it a serious stress test—he was the Playboy Prince. Everyone knew that. And Playboy Princes didn't magically change their stripes just because they were married. Genetics were not on his side. The best way to prevent another royal divorce was simply not to get married in the first place.

Which meant no wife and no children, and he was content with that. One of his cousins, or one of their many offspring, could inherit the throne. He also had no wish to bring into the world a child who would endure the same loveless, stilted childhood that he'd had. Who would watch one parent flirt with every female staff member. Watch the other slowly drink herself into oblivion.

Simone got up and moved around the small kitchen. He studied her back as she assembled a plate with some bread, cheese and hummus. Her movements were fluid, her curves hypnotising and very watchable. Though that could have been the transatlantic trip catching up with him.

She put the plate on the coffee table.

'A feast,' he said.

'Don't joke. I wasn't expecting to eat here myself, let alone entertain royalty.'

'It's great, and honestly I'm not very hungry.'

She looked at him as if she didn't believe him. She knew him too well.

'We can order something in if you like. This isn't exactly up to my mother's standard.'

Alea, an acclaimed chef, had stayed working for the King even after everything that had happened between the two of them. Ed had never been able to work out why, but he conceded there were many things he was destined never to understand about romantic relationships.

They ate the food and drank the rest of the wine. 'The bookshop is great. Truly. Why a bookshop?'

'I've always loved reading. But more than that I've always loved sharing books. A big part of my business is helping people track down out-of-print books. The bookshop is just one part of the business. Much of what I do is online.'

The certainty she had about her ambition was inspiring. He'd had no idea growing up that this was her dream. 'When did you realise this was what you wanted to do?

'Not long after I was sent away. Banished.'

'You weren't banished.'

'Yes, I was.'

'You were sent away for your own protection.'

She scoffed. 'My protection? It was a bit late for that.'

'Yes. Your protection. In case anyone found out.'

It was strange that she didn't remember, but it

had been a strange and stressful time. His father had grown very close to Simone's mother gradually over the years. As their affair had developed the King, Alea and the other staff had been anxious to protect Simone from any fallout and his father had paid for Simone's boarding school fees. Ed suspected that having Simone out of the apartment had suited his father as much as his professed motive of protecting her from scandal.

Simone had jumped at the chance to leave the palace and study in Switzerland, and Ed hadn't realised at the time that it would mean that Simone would never return to live in Florena again.

'But they did find out. The video got out,' Simone said.

'What video?'

Ed's stomach dropped. It had been a day of earth-shattering scandals in his family, but he was sure he'd have remembered a video of the King and Simone's mother.

'What video? The one of me embarrassing myself in front of everyone at your seventeenth.'

Ed rubbed his eyes. It was early afternoon in New York and he'd missed a whole night's sleep. But he must be more exhausted than he realised.

He didn't remember any video from his seventeenth, but when he saw Simone's mouth fall open he stopped and, fortunately, had enough sense not to blurt out the first thing on his mind.

Was it possible that Simone didn't know about

the affair his father and her mother had conducted for at least a year?

No. That would be absurd. She must have known.

Simone had been sent away to school. Not only to protect her from any fallout if the affair became known but also to hide it from her. Was it possible her mother—nor anyone else for that matter—had never told her? Was it possible she'd never figured it out?

CHAPTER THREE

WAS HE SERIOUS? How could he have forgotten about the video? *What video? The* video. The one that had ruined her life. Shaped the course of everything that had come after it. The single most embarrassing, frightening and heartbreaking moment of her life.

'This is not the time to joke,' she said.

He held up his hands. 'I'm not joking.'

'You're seriously telling me you don't know about the video of me making a fool of myself at your party?'

He looked genuinely pained with confusion, his green eyes wide and innocent.

'I honestly have no idea. What video? Please tell me.'

'I don't want to talk about it.'

She crossed her arms. If he didn't remember she didn't want to enlighten him. That would be like reliving the whole horrible experience again.

She had devised a plan. To her deluded, infatuated, teenage brain it had seemed like the perfect plan.

Ed had been about to turn seventeen and in one more year would go abroad to university. His head was beginning to be turned by the glamorous young women who had constantly been thrown into his path. He'd been growing particularly close to a girl called Morgane, the daughter of friends of his parents. Morgane had always been finding some excuse to visit him at the palace.

The world had been at Ed's feet. If he was ever going to love Simone she had known it had to be then. Before he saw too much of the world and realised that she, provincial Simone, who had never even left Florena, was not good enough for a prince. It had been then or never.

Her dilemma had been that if she told Ed she loved him and he didn't feel the same way she'd jeopardise their friendship. So she had devised a way to let him know she loved him without actually making a declaration. Plausible deniability and all that. She'd decided she would sing to him, and if he loved her too he'd think the song was about him. He'd come to her and they would fall into each other's arms and be together for ever and ever.

Simone had helped Ed and his assistant organise the party. They'd chosen a nineteen-eighties theme, with arcade games, glo-sticks and, most importantly, karaoke.

Her plan had been much more subtle than actually coming straight out and saying, *Ed, I'm in love with you.* But if he felt the same way surely he'd understand what she was saying.

Best-laid plans and all that… The sound system hadn't been terrific. And it hadn't helped that she'd chosen a song that stretched even the best singers in the world—*I Will Always Love You*, the Dolly Parton/Whitney Houston classic.

It had turned out that Simone's voice sounded different in the summer house than it did in the shower.

There had been laughter and sniggers. Ed hadn't laughed, but he hadn't said anything either, being too busy talking to Morgane all night.

He hadn't returned her feelings. But, she'd reasoned, as she'd cried into her pillow that night, at least she hadn't come right out and told him. Heartbreak was bad enough without the other person knowing how much they'd hurt you. At least she hadn't had to face the pain of having him reject her to her face.

She had decided she would get a good night's sleep and in the morning Ed would have forgotten all about it.

But the next day it had been everywhere.

All over social media and the front page of the newspaper, the *Daily Florenan*. She'd been made into a hashtag, for crying out loud.

And cry she had. Alone in her room. All that day and into the next.

And the things they'd written about her. The comments on the video had been merciless. All of them mean. Some dark. A few telling her to end her life.

She'd been a sixteen-year-old kid.

The next day her mother had come to her room and asked how she felt about going to school in Switzerland for a semester. Simone had never heard a plan that sounded so good. She'd known she was being sent away in disgrace, but she hadn't cared,

One semester had turned into six, and she'd never had to live in Florena again.

She swirled the stem of her wine glass, hoping Ed would change the subject.

But he pressed on. 'Do you know why you went to boarding school?'

She scoffed. 'Of course I know. Do *you* know?'

He nodded.

'Then I don't know why we're even talking about this.'

She tore off a piece of bread and loaded it up heavily with hummus. Two hours ago she'd been happily going about her life, but now Ed was making himself at home on her couch, digging up old memories and picking at her emotional wounds.

'So tell me,' she said. 'Why do you think I left?'

'No, no. You first.'

She took a swig of wine. She might as well tell the story first. Her way.

'You remember your seventeenth birthday?'

'Yes, I was there.'

The grin he gave her almost made her stop talking. He was impossible. Gorgeous and utterly, completely impossible. She looked at the spot on the wall where the paint was peeling rather than looking at his sparkly, teasing green eyes.

'There were lots of people at the party. Friends of yours. Friends of your parents.'

'And you.'

'Yeah.'

Did he remember what she'd been wearing? A red dress chosen specially that had been at the absolute top of her budget. Still not as fancy as the couture worn by some of the other guests. Did he remember how her hair had looked? Sleek and straightened and shinier than it had been before or since.

No. He did not.

Still, if he didn't remember the dress or the hair, maybe he didn't remember the singing.

'It was in the summer house…' she said.

'Nineteen-eighties theme. We hired Space Invaders machines,' he added.

He did remember. Some of it at least.

She drew a deep breath. 'And I, being a stupid sixteen-year-old, thought it would be a good idea to sing.'

He didn't speak. He just let her keep talking.

'I chose the wrong song. And I made a mess of it.'

'It wasn't that bad.'

'Thank you for saying that, but we both know it was. And I was destroyed.'

'Destroyed? By whom?'

'By the world! Everyone on social media. I was a hashtag.'

His eyes were blank, jaw slack.

'You don't remember?'

'Of course I do. I just didn't think it was that bad.'

'Not that bad?' Ed might have been oblivious to what her gesture meant, but the rest of the world hadn't. They had all deduced correctly that she'd been trying to serenade him.

'Sim, sweetheart. I had no idea you felt this way about it.'

'Well, it was awful. I was hashtag *palaceserenade*.'

'Please don't think for a second that I'm trying to diminish or dismiss what you went through, but I do understand.'

She crossed her arms.

Ed leant towards her, his green eyes holding hers in a caring gaze. For a moment she thought he might lift his hand and brush her cheek. Simone pulled her gaze away from his.

Don't fall. Don't fall.

'As someone who's been the subject of many hashtags, and more than his fair share of memes, I do understand. And what I've learnt is that the rest of the world never thinks as much about you as you think they do. I bet no one in Florena even remembers it.'

'Oh, they do.'

Each time Simone visited Florena the trolls would somehow find her. Once a photo of her in a supermarket had made it onto social media. Another time a photo of her and Alea in a café had done the rounds. With the usual number of hateful messages, comments and threats.

She wasn't a celebrity. She had been a sixteen-year-old girl at a private party. The trolls still came after her. She'd been such a liability to the palace she'd been sent away to boarding school. Ed could be blasé about it—he was always in the public eye—but he could handle it. She didn't have that kind of strength.

'Really? I'd almost forgotten.'

He had completely forgotten. Because he'd barely noticed in the first place. He'd forgotten because his life had moved on. But that video was still on the internet. With all the vile comments.

'It's different for you,' she said.

'Why? Because I'm a prince? Does that make me immune from mockery? Laughter?' He placed his wine glass down and stood. 'Maybe I should go.'

Oh, no. This wasn't what she'd meant.

She stood too and reached for his arm. 'Ed, no. Please. I'm sorry. It was insensitive of me.'

It was only then, once he was looking down at her hand gripping his, that she realised how close she was to him. And how outrageously strong his biceps felt under her grip.

'Ed, please stay.'

He nodded. 'I know you didn't mean it. I know it *is* different for me. I have the protection of the palace. I've been trained to cope. And you were only sixteen. Besides, you should've been safe in the palace. It was meant to be a private party.'

She nodded.

Growing up, he had confided in her many times about the intrusiveness of photographers. About how it felt to have his every move scrutinised. He was fortunate that his parents had made sure he had been supported, counselled and given techniques to manage the peculiar psychological stressors that came with being a prince.

'I'm sorry.' She gave his arm another gentle squeeze. Damn, it felt good. If only she could slide her hand up to his shoulder, slip it around his neck and…

Ed shook his head. 'No, I'm sorry. I didn't realise how much it had affected you.'

'Well, yes, one stupid song changed my life. But I suppose if I hadn't been filmed I wouldn't have had to leave Florena and then I wouldn't live here.'

She threw her arms wide. She loved her apartment, her bookshop and her life in Paris.

The look he returned was unreadable, but the way he twisted his body just enough to free himself from her touch spoke volumes. They were both upset but he couldn't leave. And she didn't want him to leave like this.

She poured them both another glass of wine and he sat. They settled in for an evening of chatting about his travels and work and her bookshop, the books they'd been reading, the podcasts they had been listening to. Avoiding talk of palace gossip and their teenage years.

Eventually, when her eyelids were drooping, he

said, 'You should go to bed. You have to work to-morrow, I assume.'

She nodded. 'Do you want the bed? I'll take the couch.'

'I won't accept it. You're the one doing me the favour.'

'But the couch is tiny. Barely big enough for me.'

'Which is exactly why I won't let you take it.'

He could share your bed.

And what if her hands had a life of their own in the middle of the night? What if her unconscious self couldn't help sliding over to his side of the bed? How would she explain that?

'Wait a minute. Do you have any bags? Were you travelling with anyone?' Simone asked.

'I left the airport right away—as soon as I saw the message from Father. My valet took everything and went on to Florena.'

'So you have nothing?'

He looked down at his backpack. 'A toothbrush but not much else. It'll be okay. I'll have a call to return home by the morning.'

It would only be one night.

'We could share?'

The air was suddenly as thick as her voice sounded.

Her heart beat hard in her chest several times before he answered, 'Are you sure?'

'We've slept together before.'

His mouth dropped.

'When we were kids,' she said. 'Sleepovers, sleep-outs!'

'It's not quite the same thing.' He spoke slowly, carefully.

She'd gone too far. 'We're just friends. We might be a little older. But we're still just friends.'

If she kept saying it enough it might eventually become true.

He didn't speak for a very long time—so long that she was sure her cheeks must be the colour of a stop sign.

'Are you sure?' he asked.

She exhaled. 'I think I can manage to keep my hands off you,' she joked.

He leant towards her. Close enough that she could feel the heat from his body. He stared at her. Raised one eyebrow.

'What if I can't?'

He didn't smile, and a whoosh swept through her body.

The thought of Ed not being able to keep his hands off her was absurd. So why wasn't he laughing?

She looked into the depths of his eyes, so closely she could see the flecks of gold. And something else. Suddenly each breath felt as if she was dragging bricks into her lungs. There was no oxygen in the air, and something was pressing on her chest.

He turned his head and cleared his throat. 'I'm just worried your snoring will keep me awake.'

He smiled and the spell was broken.

Simone bumped his upper arm gently. 'I doubt you'll be able to hear my snoring over your own.'

She grabbed her pyjamas and changed in the bathroom. She washed her face and brushed her teeth—her usual evening routine, but it felt so strange with Ed being just outside the door. Ed Berringer was in her attic. His tall, athletic frame was sprawled on her small bed.

Oh, Ed... It was so much easier to forget him and push her feelings to one side than it was to face them. She managed when she wasn't near him. When he was simply an idea, not a living, breathing man. But tonight he was a living, breathing, beautiful man who was going to sleep in her bed.

No. She'd got over Ed once before. She was not going to put herself through that again.

Climbing carefully into bed so as not to bump him, she said, 'Will you be able to sleep?

'Eventually. I need to get back onto European time anyway. Thanks again.'

'You don't have to thank me. You're welcome any time. I'm glad you felt you could come to me.'

The smile he gave her melted every single muscle in her heart.

Don't fall. Don't fall.

It was just a childish crush and she'd made herself get over it once before.

She was about to turn and begin what would surely be a restless night when she remembered.

'Wait. Why did you think I was sent away from Florena?'

'Oh, just that… The song. The video.'

'Really? But you mentioned an affair?'

'Yes. The hashtag *palaceserenade* affair.'

She sighed. That was all he meant.

She could feel him shuffling next to her, trying to make himself comfortable. She turned out her bedside light and the room fell into darkness.

'Goodnight, Ed.'

'Goodnight, Sim. I hope the foxes don't get you.'

She smiled. They had camped out a few times in the palace garden one summer. They had put up a tent and toasted marshmallows on a small camp stove. They had made a pact to stay up all night, but they'd fallen asleep in the early hours, exhausted. They must have been nine or ten maybe.

'Do you remember when we camped in the garden?'

'Of course. We did it a few times. I was so lucky to have you growing up. And now. I know we haven't seen much of each other lately, but I really do think of you like family,' he said into the darkness.

She sighed.

He thinks of you as a sister.

Eventually his breathing became steadier and deeper. She knew he was asleep.

He wasn't in her bed by choice, only by circumstance. She didn't want something to happen between them simply because she was the nearest warm body. Besides, her and Ed was impossible. The last thing she wanted was to return to Florena and its hateful press. The last thing she wanted was to face the scrutiny that would come from dating Prince Edouard the Playboy Prince.

She chanted this to herself over and over, before she finally fell asleep.

CHAPTER FOUR

ED OPENED THE windows and the sounds of the street floated in. Snatches of conversation, cutlery clinking on plates, a television in another language and over it all the contented hum of the city. Below him the street was already bustling with Parisians going about their day. Including Simone.

He wasn't sure when she had left as he'd been in a deep, deep sleep. Exhaustion, jetlag and maybe one too many glasses of wine had thankfully, meant he'd slept soundly. Now he was awake the real nightmare began again.

There were no messages from either of his parents and neither answered his calls.

He located the coffee machine in the small kitchen, and brewed himself a cup.

He scrolled through his tablet as he drank his coffee and searched for the most recent press about his father. He'd tried calling his father's advisers, but those who answered told him they knew nothing. He should be back in Florena, showing support for his father. Being the respectable face of the monarchy.

Ha! Respectable! No wonder his father wanted him to stay away.

Ed was far from innocent. Though he was hardly as promiscuous as the tabloids would have people believe. Maybe about a tenth of their reports about him had any substance.

Still, his name was almost never printed without the words 'The Playboy Prince' preceding it. Ed enjoyed a party as much as the next single thirty-year-old, but he wasn't amoral. He'd never cheated on anyone because he'd never stayed with any woman long enough for it to be an issue. If his father couldn't stay faithful, if his grandfather couldn't stay faithful, what made Ed think he could? It was much simpler not to marry.

He wasn't the falling in love type. Just like his father and grandfather. Ed's duty was to his country first and foremost. While he was young Ed was travelling the world promoting Florena and its economic interests. A life in the air left no time for serious relationships. And in the future—hopefully many years in the future—he intended to fulfil his role as King alone.

That way he could avoid the type of scandals that had plagued his forefathers. Loveless marriages inevitably led to infidelities, unhappiness and scandal. Not to mention unhappy children who didn't understand why their parents only spoke to one another sarcastically, if they even bothered to speak to one another at all.

Apart from dating, which as far as he knew wasn't a crime, he was a respectable person. He'd studied diligently and worked hard. He treated everyone with respect and avoided trouble. He had done everything expected of him as a prince. And he'd done it well. Which was why it went against every fibre of his being to stay here and not return home to help figure out a way through this mess.

You could just leave. Get on the next flight.

He could, but his father had ordered him to stay away. His king had told him to stay where he was. So he must.

Besides, going home would mean leaving Simone. He wasn't ready to do that. His instinct to come here had been spot-on. Last night had been calm. He could relax with her. Say exactly what he was thinking and feeling. With her, the troubles and worries seemed that much further away. If he couldn't be in Florena this was where he wanted to be.

He flicked on the small television. The news channel had his father's news rotating across the ticker tape every five minutes or so, simply described as 'a disgrace'.

Ed held degrees in government and international affairs. He spoke several languages. Why didn't his father want him in Florena?

He looked down at his clothes. The same outfit he'd been in for over twenty-four hours now. He looked up 'clothing delivery Paris'. If he bought a change of clothes and other supplies his father was bound to summon him home immediately. He ordered some clothes and pyjamas from his favourite designer and paid for an urgent delivery.

But the call from the palace didn't come.

A noise outside the window caught his attention. A black cat was on the window ledge, meowing to come in. Belle. He opened the window and the cat jumped inside. She weaved between his legs and he stroked her behind the ears.

To his mind, there were three main ways this could play out. First, his father might decide to divorce his mother and marry Celine and weather the fallout. Second, Laurent might insist he put the question of the monarchy to the people as a vote. Ed wasn't sure how that would play out. Even a narrow win for the monarchy would still feel like a loss.

But there was a third possibility. The worst possibility of all. One he didn't dare think about.

Abdication.

Ed knew he would be King— he'd been training his whole life for it and had made his peace with it. But not yet.

And not like this.

The journalist on the television was interviewing a woman who was saying that the most important person in the whole royal scandal was the unborn child. Once upon a time he'd wanted a sibling, and then Simone had come along. That little girl he'd stumbled across one morning in the garden, tossing a ball to Suzette, his dog. They had played for hours and later he had thanked his parents for getting him a sister.

They'd laughed mercilessly. 'Oh, darling. She's with the staff. She's not your sister.'

But if they'd thought she was beneath him they hadn't seemed to mind that Simone had kept him occupied. They hadn't seemed to notice the hours and hours he'd spent with her in the palace kitchens, or in Simone's apartment, eating with her, watching television, playing games, because neither of them had seemed to notice anything he did unless he got into trouble.

Ed had seen Simone irregularly since she'd gone away to school, because of his study, travels and work. He shouldn't have taken her friendship for granted. He should have visited this apartment before now. Made more of an effort to see her whenever he was in Paris.

He had been busy with his studying, his job and other official business. And other women. But it was also true that he had taken her, his oldest and dearest friend, for granted.

It was hard to shake away the guilt. While neglecting his best friend wasn't as bad as anything his father had done, it still wasn't the behaviour of the man he wanted to be.

Ed pulled out his phone and searched for the video she had claimed was the reason she'd been sent to boarding school. A video he had pretended to remember, but in reality had no recollection of.

He searched for hashtag *palaceserenade*, certain that there would be no results. But there it was. There *she* was. A sixteen-year-old Simone, belting out 'I Will Always Love You'. She didn't have a bad voice, but it was a difficult song for anyone. Let alone a kid in a room full of people whom he saw were jeering her. But she held her head high and kept going through it all.

His heart ached for the sixteen-year-old. She was gorgeous. She looked different from the way she usually had back then. Her blonde hair was straightened and sleek. The red dress showing more skin than he thought a sixteen year old should.

What had possessed her to sing that song? Other people had been singing, but he didn't recall anyone taking the karaoke as seriously as Simone had. He hadn't thought about that night in years. As far as he was concerned his seventeenth birthday had been much like his sixteenth. A palace-sanctioned party with as many of his parents' friends as his own.

He watched the video a second time and then read the comments. They were pretty horrible, and would have been devastating to read as a sixteen-year-old. But those comments and that video were not the reasons his father had paid for Simone's boarding school fees or her university tuition. Did she really think he would have done that over one video?

He watched it a third time and smiled. Sixteen-year-old Simone might have been mortified, but he'd bet if she watched it now, at twenty-nine years old, she'd marvel at the courage of that girl. At how gorgeous she looked.

He paused the video and looked at the frozen frame.

She doesn't know about the affair my father and

her mother conducted. She probably thinks her mother paid her school fees.

He could understand Simone not knowing at the time, his father had been discreet, but surely at some point someone would have told her.

He looked at sixteen-year-old Simone, frozen in time. Saw the dreamy look in her beautiful eyes.

Was it his place to tell her about the affair? Probably not. It wasn't his secret to tell.

The only thing he did know was that he wanted to see her. Not the sixteen-year-old, but the beautiful twenty-nine-year-old woman downstairs, going about her day. Running her own business in one of the most beautiful parts of the world.

You could go downstairs.

And be seen? No. He pulled out his laptop. There was a day's worth of emails to catch up on. He was still the Crown Prince and Trade Envoy and had responsibilities. He set to work.

Simone didn't know what she'd expected to find when she went back upstairs that evening. But it wasn't baking.

Her apartment smelt of her mother. Of home. The source of the aroma—a plate of madeleines fresh from the oven—sat on her kitchen table.

'Are you trying to make me homesick?'

'Why? Have I?'

Simone turned her head so he wouldn't see the tears welling in her eyes. She closed her eyes and breathed in deeply. To steady herself and banish the tears. The madeleines reminded her of her mother. She missed her deeply. So much it made her ache. They spoke most days, and Alea came to Paris whenever she could. She loved it as much as Simone, and not living in the same city was hard.

'I take it you haven't heard from the palace?'

He shook his head.

'I'm sorry.'

Simone reached over and touched his shoulder. He was wearing a soft cashmere sweater and felt warm and delicious under her touch. Her hand tingled and the sensation spread up her arm. He lifted his own hand and placed it on hers, rubbing it slightly.

If only she could move closer and slip her hand all the way across his shoulders. Slide into his lap and…

'I'm sure they know you care,' she said, trying to string a sentence together even though her body was bursting with sparks.

'You're stuck with me a little longer.'

'I told you—you can stay as long as you need.'

She took her hand away with regret, because if she didn't do it now she just might slide it up to his neck, into his soft hair and…

She had to change the subject. 'I can't believe you baked. And madeleines!'

He passed her one and she took it gratefully.

Sweet, with just the right amount of softness and chewiness.

'It's the only thing I know how to bake. Your mother taught me.'

Simone remembered a twelve-year-old Ed, always begging for the biscuits and watching Alea make them. Simone marvelled that Ed had actually remembered how to bake them. Just like her mother's.

You're older now. Stronger. You can do this.

He looked up, their eyes met, and her stomach swooped. This was bad. Very bad. As a kid her affection for him had been innocent. She'd adored him, but when her mind had leapt forward to what might happen if they should ever actually kiss she hadn't known what would happen next. Everything after a chaste, Disney-movie-like kiss had been unknown to her.

She hadn't experienced deep physical desire until she'd come to Paris. Since then she'd gravitated to men who looked nothing like Ed, and had several fulfilling physical relationships. She'd convinced herself she was really physically attracted to a different sort of man, and that her feelings for Ed were platonic only.

'You got some new clothes,' she remarked. 'Thank goodness. I didn't want to say anything, but the smell...' She held her nose and waved her hand.

He laughed—as well he might. Despite his wearing the same outfit for twenty-four hours, there was nothing she found off-putting about his scent at all. And now, with fresh baking and a freshly showered and changed Ed, her apartment had never smelt as good.

Careful, Simone. Careful.

This was good. Banter. Teasing. Like when they were kids. Before she'd been swamped with adolescent hormones and decided she had a crush on him. If she teased him he wouldn't realise how close she was to burying her face in his neck.

'And there's more.'

Ed stepped to one side and revealed an eclectic feast. Fresh bread, cheese and a bottle of Burgundy. He lifted the lid off the casserole dish on top of the stove to reveal a simmering chicken casserole.

'You made coq au vin? How?'

'Is it still your favourite?'

'Do you expect me to believe you cooked this?'

'Why couldn't I cook this?'

She levelled him with a look.

'Okay, you've got me on the casserole. It was pre-prepared. I didn't think you'd thank me if I made it.'

She laughed.

'But I did bake.'

She nodded. That she believed.

'I wanted to thank you. For letting me impose another night.'

Another night. In the same bed as Ed. It was just as well he'd shown some appreciation for what he was putting her body through.

Before she realised what was happening, his large hand enveloped hers—warm and secure. His thumb brushed against her wrist and her body swayed.

'I'm very grateful. I know we haven't seen much of one another lately, and I know I'm putting you out. But I'm very glad I'm here with you.'

She looked into his eyes. They were earnest and serious. Deep and soulful.

Don't fall. Don't fall.

'It's been an awful few days and there is no one else who understands me quite like you do.'

Their faces were a mere foot away from one another's. If she didn't move now she'd reveal too much.

She shook her head and turned, so she didn't make a fool of herself.

As she turned she noticed the vase on the coffee table.

Flowers. The vase on her small table was filled with pink peonies.

It's a centrepiece for a table. He hasn't bought you flowers.

But it felt as if he had. And he'd baked her madeleines. And bought her wine.

Ed pulled out her chair. It hit the bookcase behind, but she didn't mind. Sitting in her cramped apartment with her prince was the only place in the world she wanted to be.

CHAPTER FIVE

BEING A PRINCE was not the endless lark everyone thought it was. On days like this it was positively tedious. Did anyone else have to worry so much about public perceptions that they would agree to be trapped in a Parisian turret for twenty-four hours?

The only communication he'd had from either of his parents in the past twenty-four hours had been a brief message from his father's private secretary thanking him for his patience and telling him his father would speak to him soon. He'd tried to get some work done, even attempted a video conference, but he hadn't been able to concentrate. His thoughts kept drifting to his father and his mother. And then Simone.

Baking was a type of procrastination that was entirely new to him, but it had worked. And, best of all, he'd made Simone happy.

Simone sat, closed her eyes and groaned as she breathed in the food. The sight did something strange to his chest. The steam from the coq au vin rose around her face, leaving a gentle glisten across her skin.

She grabbed a handful of hair from the nape of her neck and twisted it back from her face so she could eat without it falling in front of her, revealing the smooth skin behind her ears. He bit down the desire to kiss it.

How had he never noticed how gorgeous she was?

They hadn't seen a lot of each other in the past few years, but even so. Now that he'd noticed it was difficult to believe he hadn't before.

Maybe it was just familiarity. She reminded him of happy times. Of childhood. Of feeling secure.

She was a best friend.

Except…not.

Now she was an independent woman, running a business in one of the world's most popular cities. The woman sitting across from him now, with her eyes half-closed, groaning gratefully as she ate the meal he'd procured.

You've actually never noticed her lips before. Pink. Plump. Perfect…

He shook his head.

'How was your afternoon?' he asked.

'Good. We had lots of traffic. And I managed to track down some sought-after first editions for some buyers.'

'Do you have any help in the bookshop?'

'A few casuals. My friend André helps out if I get really stuck.'

André. Ed's back straightened.

'His girlfriend, Julia, is my best friend.'

Ed felt his muscles relax.

'But you still work seven days? That's a lot.'

'I want to own this place, and that takes hard work.'

He drew breath, about to ask her how much money

she needed, but she raised her hand before he could get half a word out.

'I need to do this by myself—and I can. Mum's offered to help, but I don't want to accept. She's done so much for me, especially putting me through school, helping me out when I first came to Paris.'

'Your mum's terrific. But did she really pay your school fees?'

He had to tread carefully. But he also had to know what she knew. While it wasn't his secret to tell, it didn't feel right that he knew something like this when Simone didn't.

Simone looked up. 'What do you mean?'

'It was an exclusive school. Your mother did well to afford it.'

'Who else would have?'

'I… That is… I wondered if my parents might have.'

The creases on Simone's gorgeous face deepened. 'Why would they?'

'Can you not think of a reason?'

She laid down her cutlery and crossed her arms.

'No. And I don't think Mum would have accepted. Besides, my father left her some money. Not a lot. But enough. We're not royalty, but she's not poor.'

He was now certain that Simone didn't know about the affair. But she was certainly suspicious.

'Ed… What do you know?'

'Nothing. I'm sorry. It was very rude of me to

question you. I've had a strange and privileged life and sometimes I make assumptions I shouldn't.'

And sometimes I don't shut my mouth when I should.

Their parents' affair wasn't his secret to tell, but not telling felt as if he was betraying her. Half the palace or more knew about his father and her mother. Was it right that Simone didn't?

'My business is great. I don't need any help.'

He frowned. 'But you're working seven days a week.'

'Because I want to! I love my job,' she insisted, in a way that indicated the conversation was over.

They ate in silence a while longer. He tried to think of something else to talk about, but drew a blank.

He looked out of the window at the city lights. He hadn't expected to be staying a second night here and had assumed he'd be back in Florena by now.

'I'm sorry for imposing on you.'

'I've told you I don't mind.'

'I didn't mean to imprison myself in your apartment.'

She laughed. 'You're not a prisoner. Not really. You're free to leave any time. It's your loyalty to your father that's keeping you here.'

She smiled at him, and her compliment warmed his chest.

There were worse places to be trapped. Though it would've been nice to be somewhere more spacious. Maybe with a pool. Or some sunshine. But at least he was trapped with Simone.

'I'm sure it won't be for much longer,' she said.

He shook his head. The silence from the palace said so many things. Was his father contemplating a press blackout or something else entirely?

A prisoner. The look on Ed's face was heartbreaking. Ed had never really struggled with his destiny or his duty. He saw it as an honour, not a burden. Simone had no idea how Ed would cope if his role were taken away from him. Some people were suited to a life of duty and Ed was one of them.

Simone was not. As a child she had adored living in the palace. Adored catching glimpses of the Queen all dressed up for a night out. Or even a night in. Young Simone had once thought it was the life she wanted. But that had been before hashtag *palaceserenade*. Before the worst of the internet had rained down on her.

'I don't know how you do it,' she said now.

'Do what?'

'Put up with everyone knowing who you are and commenting on you.'

'I wouldn't wish it on anyone.'

Her heart dropped. She knew she would never even date Ed. Let alone marry him. Her body shouldn't be reacting like this to something she'd always known was true.

Besides, apart from proving to her that Ed didn't

love her, the whole hashtag *palaceserenade* non-sense had shown her that she didn't have what it took to be in the public eye anyway.

'But some people don't choose to be famous,' she said. 'It just happens because of circumstance.'

He looked at her closely and she felt her skin burn. Did he know what she was saying?

'You have to learn to get used to it,' he said. 'Or you break.'

'Yeah.'

She understood that. The few weeks when her video had been all over the internet had been the worst of her life. Physically leaving Florena had helped, but blocking social media had been more important. The problem was every time she'd thought it might have died down she'd check to see if people were still talking about her. She'd go on-line to check, and all the horrible things—the really toxic comments—would come across her screen.

'You can't worry over what other people say about you. You have to have a clear sense of your-self. What is real and what is not.'

They were wise words. But easier said than done.

'Do you always manage to do that?' she asked. 'To have a clear sense of yourself?'

He pulled his 'I'm thinking' face before reply-ing, 'Mostly. I don't go looking for clips about me. My staff tell me what I need to know. Otherwise I block it out.'

It was easy when you were a prince. And when

you had staff to monitor your social media presence and advise you about it. Ed had been raised with the confidence of knowing who he was and what his role in the world was. He was also being given the support to keep doing it.

'Maybe you should too,' he suggested, leaning into her.

The words were no use to her now, but would have helped when she was sixteen.

She had been a kid. She hadn't had the training he'd had. No one had explained to her how to deal with the trolls.

How had she got through it?

The school counsellor had been amazing. A wonderful woman who'd tried to instil in Simone exactly what Ed was talking about. A clear sense of herself and a disregard for what other people thought or said.

Her best friend Julia, who was not only good at hugs, but also gave great reality checks, was wonderful too. 'He's not the one for you. And you know that.'

But looking at Ed now, reclined on her couch, twirling his wine glass, she knew a small part of her wished this was her life. Their life. Working in the bookshop in the day and sharing their evenings together. Eating, drinking, talking. And later she would take his face in her hands and....

It wasn't fair that he was still her favourite person in the entire world.

* * *

Before she realised it was almost midnight. They had been talking, laughing and reminiscing about their childhoods. As the evening wore on her thoughts became more muddied, her inhibitions lowered. She stood to get them both a drink and when she returned to the sofa her weight pushed the soft cushions closer and their hips touched. Nothing like a bit of self-torture.

But when she looked at him he was smiling. Contentedly.

'There's nowhere else I'd rather be imprisoned,' he said, and lay back.

Now their shoulders were touching. The sofa really was too small for both of them. Or she'd sat too close to him. She inhaled to clear her head, but breathed him in. He smelt of her own shampoo, and damn if it didn't smell good on him.

Even if Simone did still have feelings for Ed— which she didn't—they could never go anywhere. He thought of her as a sister. Besides, she certainly wasn't going to marry a prince. Not when she'd already experienced the kind of vitriol that was reserved for women who did.

He was finishing a story about a friend he had in New York and she was only half listening. Her thoughts were preoccupied in thinking about how close their shoulders were. The way his hair curled around the back of his ear. The light stubble that was now apparent on his cheeks.

It was lucky she was holding her glass in her hands, otherwise there would be nothing stopping her placing one of them on his knee.

Giving herself a mental shakedown, she tried looking for his flaws. His annoying habits.

He sucked on his thumb when he was thinking. He blinked when he was lying. He often lost track of what he was saying and stopped speaking mid-sentence.

Damn. Even his flaws were adorable.

Simone came back from the bathroom after changing into her pyjamas. Ed tried not to study the loose fabric skimming gently over her curves. He ran his tongue around his mouth, which had suddenly gone dry. She eyed his new pyjamas—another of today's purchases.

'You'll be wanting your own cupboard space soon,' she said.

He was glad she kept joking. It was what they did. They *didn't* stare into one another's eyes for long, uncomfortable moments.

They climbed into their respective sides of the bed and when they were settled she reached over and switched off the bedside light. Ambient light crept in from the street but otherwise they were in darkness. They lay on their backs, looking at the ceiling.

Last night, exhausted from his trip and with more than enough wine in his stomach, he had fallen asleep easily. But tonight… He wasn't sure how he would fall asleep as long as he could feel Simone's gorgeous weight in the bed next to him. They weren't even touching, but he could feel her in his bones and in his pores.

What if he pretended to sleep and accidentally rolled in her direction? What then?

She'll push you back to your side of the bed or get up and go to the sofa.

Simone had invited him into her bed platonically. He couldn't throw himself at her.

'What if I can't keep my hands off you…?'

Last night he'd said it as a joke. Tonight it didn't feel like a joke at all.

Each time one of them moved he was careful to keep the space between them. For her sake more than his. He knew that if their bodies collided he'd be at risk of coming completely undone.

So he endured. As still as he could. Wound tighter than tight. Listening to her breathing become heavy and regular. But even then sleep evaded him.

His thoughts of Simone were confusing, to say the least. Upsetting at worst. Had she always been this beautiful and he'd just failed to see? Or had she been transformed somehow because he was trapped with her.

Excuses aside, he knew the truth. She was beautiful and always had been. He just hadn't noticed because she was his friend, and friends didn't think about friends like that. But now he had noticed the pink of her lips, the blush of colour across her cheekbones, the sound of her laugher.

It was seeing her here—in her home—in Paris. Thriving. Planning to buy her own business and apartment. He realised, with an uncomfortable lump in his chest, that she belonged here now and not in Florena. A sense of loss swept through him. He longed for her to be by his side. And not just as his friend. He longed to be even closer to her than they were now, with their bodies lying mere inches apart.

No. He told himself that he was being silly. The sensations his body was experiencing when he thought about Simone were happening just because of the immense amount of stress he was under.

The longer he lay awake and pondered, the more he realised that it didn't matter why he was seeing her differently. The better question was what he was going to do about it.

The answer, he knew, was absolutely nothing. She was his best friend. The person he was depending on. The relationship he most wanted to treasure and nurture.

Rolling over and sliding his palm over her soft curves was not even an option. Putting his arms around her and pulling her to him was out of the question. Taking her rosy lips against his and tasting their sweetness was unthinkable.

Not to mention arrogant.

What made him think she would even welcome

such a move? She was happy in Paris. He was a friend from her past and had no role to play in her future.

And this was hardly the time for him to do anything that would get his private life into the public realm.

So these new feelings and desires were just a blip. An aberration. Once he was home and no longer trapped here their lives would go on as they were meant to.

Separately.

Besides, he wasn't here as Simone's prisoner, but as her guest. If anyone was keeping him prisoner it was his father.

Around two a.m. Ed carefully reached for his phone, in the vague hope there would be a message, but his home screen was blank.

Simone rolled over and a wave of her scent reached his nose. She smelt like summer in the garden at the palace and his muscles clenched even tighter.

She was comfort and home all rolled into one. That was all it was, he told himself as he lay stiffly in the dark, trying his best to keep still. He hadn't anticipated the longing he'd feel to roll over and pull her close. Hadn't anticipated how many times he'd come so close to doing so.

He contemplated getting out of bed and going back to the sofa to cool down. But his limbs were heavy and the thought of leaving Simone was even less appealing than the risk that he might roll into her.

He brought his breath in time with hers and finally fell asleep.

Ed had no idea how many hours later he woke up. The curtains were flung open and the sunlight streamed in brightly, exposing everything.

Simone handed him a cup of takeaway coffee.

'You're a goddess,' he replied, eagerly inhaling the smell of the fresh brew.

The words escaped his lips before he could think twice, but he wasn't wrong. Her golden hair caught the morning sun and his breath with it. He couldn't read the look that passed across her face. Confu sion? Annoyance? He should probably try to rein in these new strange feelings. Especially since he was already imposing so much on her. On her life. On her bed. He couldn't repay her generosity by hitting on her.

'I'm afraid you might need something stronger than a coffee,' she said. 'You need to watch this.'

Simone picked up the television remote and turned on the news.

'What is it?' he asked.

'It's better if you just see.'

It didn't take long for the report Simone was referring to to come back through the news cycle. The Prime Minister of Florena, Pierre Laurent, was giving a press conference. He was standing on the steps outside the Parliament building. While the crowd of journalists was not massive, it was big enough.

'The citizens of Florena have had enough. This is not the behaviour we expect or deserve from our monarch. This isn't the Middle Ages. This is the twenty-first century. The way in which the King has disrespected his wife, Queen Isabella, is not the way we expect our sovereign to treat women.'

Ed couldn't help snorting. Prime Minister Laurent had been divorced a few years ago after having an affair with his secretary. For him to throw allegations of inappropriate behaviour against the King was a little rich.

'But we know it isn't just the King. We know his brother left Florena several decades ago after embezzling funds from the Government. And the King's father, the former Prince Edouard, whose premature death was notorious...'

Ed groaned. His grandfather had taken a drug overdose at the age of thirty-five, before Ed had been born. He had been in a hotel in the Bahamas with two young women who were barely out of their teens.

The allegation against his uncle was fair, but Uncle Louis hadn't set foot in Florena for years.

The allegations against Ed's grandfather were, unfortunately, true, but he'd been dead for nearly forty years.

The money the Queen had brought with her to the marriage had restored the private fortune of the royal family, and Ed's father had spent the last four decades reigning over and representing Florena with success. This was his father's first indiscretion. His first public one, at least.

'The stench of this family runs deep,' Laurent continued. *'Every Florenan knows the story* The Cursed Kingdom, *but this royal family has not learnt anything from that fairy tale. They are determined to ruin us all.'*

The Cursed Kingdom! Now he was citing an old children's story. This man was the limit.

'Dignity—that's all we expect from our monarch. He's not expected to run the country. He doesn't have to make the hard decisions.'

The Prime Minister straightened his own jacket as he said this.

Ed had feared the election of Laurent as Prime Minister would be bad for the country and he was not happy to be right.

'I think it's time Florena joined the twenty-first century.' Laurent continued.

'Oh, spare me the republican speech,' Ed yelled at the television.

Simone shook her head. 'It's worse than that.'

'We could be stronger if we joined with another, larger country. We need to have a serious discussion about whether it is sensible or viable to do this. I have been having discussions with the French Government...'

'What?' Ed stood quickly, nearly spilling his coffee.

'It doesn't make economic sense to keep our nation as a microstate...'

'Microstate!' Ed yelled. 'We're nearly as big as Belgium.'

'The geopolitical reality is that we need the protection of a larger country.'

Simone stood back, her face creased with worry. Ed grabbed his phone and pressed his father's number. To his enormous relief the King picked up right away.

'Edouard,' the King said.

'I have to come home.'

'No. Definitely not. You have to stay there. Are you somewhere safe? Somewhere private?'

'I'm with Simone. In her apartment.'

'Perfect,' replied his father.

'No! I'm no help here. I need to come home. I need to show that I support you.' He spoke too quickly and loudly, but this was the first chance he'd had to plead his case—he needed to go home.

'That's just it,' the King said. 'You need to distance yourself from me.'

'Having an affair is hardly in the same league as what Grandfather did. Or Uncle Louis.'

'That hardly matters. I don't want you getting dragged into this as well. Just stay where you are and in a few days everything will have blown over.'

Ed raked his hand through his hair. His father

was in denial. What would happen with Celine? The Queen? They needed a plan.

'No, it won't blow over. Laurent clearly has a broader agenda,' Ed insisted.

He wished he were having this conversation face to face with his father, so he could see the expression on his face and his body language.

'He's all bravado. Why would he suggest joining France when he'd just be doing himself out of a job?'

'I agree it doesn't make sense, but that's his plan.'

There was silence on the other end of the phone. And then a deep, resigned sigh. 'I wish… I wish I'd planned this better.'

You should have done a lot of things better, Ed thought.

His father had been reckless, but it was hard to blame him. He was human. Ed had known for years that his parents' marriage wasn't happy. But he'd never expected his father to be indiscreet. He'd certainly never expected his father to be caught impregnating a woman who was younger than his own son.

'The last thing we need—the last thing this country needs—is you being photographed with me.'

'But—'

'Don't argue with me, Edouard. Stay where you are. This isn't about you so don't make it about you.'

With a few words the King made him feel like a teenager again. He remembered another long-ago conversation. The one where he'd begged his father not to let Simone leave Florena.

'It's for her own good. Don't argue with me. If you care about her you will let her go.'

Ed had argued then. Pleaded with him to let Simone stay. Losing her then had been a wrench. The feelings of that day came flooding back. Pleading, arguing, and then the strange emptiness he'd felt when she was gone. A feeling that would creep up on him at unpredictable times during his adult life. A feeling he was missing something, but couldn't quite figure out what it was.

Now, knowing there was little point arguing with his father, all he said was, 'Please don't make any major decisions without talking to me.'

'You have my word.'

Ed held the silent phone in his hand. He had his father's word, but what was that worth?

'Did you hear that?' he asked Simone.

'I'm sorry. It was hard not to listen.'

He looked back to Simone, looking awkward in her own home. He wanted to go to her, pull her tight, but wasn't sure if it would be for her comfort or his. He stayed sitting on the couch.

'He wants me to keep away from it all but it feels disloyal.'

'I know it goes against every instinct you have. You want to be there. You want to do something. And it's frustrating being stuck here in this shoebox.'

He did want to be doing something, but when the

time came to leave Paris it would be with trepidation. And sadness.

'It's a nice shoebox,' he said.

She gave him a sad half-smile. 'I see where your father's coming from. If you go home…if you make some kind of statement supporting him…it could backfire.'

'How?'

'Because at his next press conference Laurent will say that since you support your father you can't be trusted either. And that Florena should sack the entire House of Berringer.'

'But how can I not support him? It looks worse if I don't, doesn't it? He's the King and he needs to stay being the King. For the sake of the country. Otherwise Laurent would have us become the smallest *department* in France.'

Simone turned and unpacked a shopping bag. She placed pastries, apples and strawberries on the small bench. 'Trust your father. I'm sure he has a plan.'

Ed wished he shared her optimism. If his father did have a plan, why would he not share it with Ed? He wasn't a kid any longer—he was trusted to manage Florena's trade relations with the United States. Why not the royal family's response to this crisis?

His muscles felt as if they might snap. First a sleepless night next to Simone and now feeling helpless and that his father didn't trust him.

'He's right, though. Laurent's plan to join France doesn't make any sense.'

'He was born here, wasn't he? Maybe he thinks it will give him a shot at running a bigger country. He thinks that if Florena is part of France he'd have a chance at being President of France.'

Ed buried his head in his hands. The man was ruthless and ambitious, but it hadn't occurred to Ed that Laurent would be so ruthless as to essentially destroy his own country to achieve that ambition. But Simone's theory made sense.

He turned back to Simone, who was preparing some of the fruit for her breakfast.

'That's quite perceptive of you.'

She laughed. 'You sound surprised.'

'I'm sorry if I do. It's been a long while since we spent so much time together.'

She shrugged. 'I follow the Florenan news.'

'You do?'

'My mum still lives there.' She drew a deep breath. 'And you.'

Her back was turned and for a moment he let his gaze rest on her. Her blonde hair was tied up in a messy bun. Her shirt dipped just low enough at the nape of her neck to reveal the soft creamy skin at the top of her back. He wanted to taste it. Lick it. He pressed his lips together.

'It's not the first time someone has discussed getting rid of the monarchy,' she said, not quite putting an end to his illicit thoughts.

The whole situation was strange. They were discussing the end of his country and all he could think about was what the skin on Simone's neck would feel like against his lips. He had to get a grip.

'Talking about a republic is one thing, but he's talking about getting rid of our whole country.'

Simone turned, putting an end to his opportunity to study her surreptitiously, and passed him a bowl of fresh fruit. Then she sat on the armchair, tucking her feet under herself, and hugged her coffee. He took the fruit gratefully. It wasn't what he would have chosen. Left to his own devices he might have taken a cap off a bottle of Scotch, but the breakfast was just what he needed. Sitting here with Simone was just what he needed. It was so much better than hearing this news alone.

'What do you think of Laurent?' he asked.

'Me?'

'Yes—you've been following the news.'

'Sure, but I've never met him. What do you make of him?'

'Ambitious. Slippery. Like most politicians. What do you think?'

'Ambitious, yes. And he likes to travel. He always seems to be visiting somewhere. And he's dating one of your old friends.'

'What? Who?'

'Oh, you know… What's her name?'

'No. I've no idea who you're talking about.'

'I thought…that is…maybe you dated her for a while? Morgane Lavigne.'

'Oh, her? I haven't seen her in years. Really? They're dating? Aren't you the fount of Florenan gossip.'

Simone shrugged. 'I keep in touch with people.'

'I'm impressed,' he said.

Simone continued to surprise him. The singing. The calmness and security of her flat. Her quirky bookshop. And her insight.

None of those things alone should have been surprising. What was rocking him, though, was the way he felt breathless when she brushed past him. The way his mind kept drifting to her. Just like his gaze, which now rested on her lips as she carefully sipped her coffee.

He knew he needed to get home to Florena as soon as possible, but when the time came he wasn't sure how he'd be able to tear himself away from Simone.

CHAPTER SIX

It was a relief to get down to the bookshop and away from Ed.

How embarrassing to mention Morgane and know she was dating the Prime Minister when Ed didn't even know that. Simone wasn't proud of it, but she did occasionally look to see what Ed's old flames were up to. Or any woman he was currently linked to.

Morgane Lavigne had often visited the palace with her parents, and had gone on several holidays with the royal family. Like Simone, Morgane had known Ed since they were children. Unlike Simone, Morgane had shared a brief relationship with Ed in their teens. She had been the person Ed had spent most of his seventeenth birthday party with. The two of them had been wrapped up in each other. Morgane had been sultry and glamorous, even as a teenager, and each time Simone had seen her she'd been monopolising Ed and Ed had never seemed to mind.

Stalking Ed's exes on the internet was not in line with Simone's strict 'No Ed' diet, but at weak moments she did relapse. Which was how she'd known about Morgane and Laurent—from some photos Morgane had posted and her vague comments about being the 'other' first lady of Florena. Morgane owned the public relations company that completed work for the government.

If she couldn't get the Prince she'd go for the Prime Minister, Simone had thought cattily, then hated herself for it and immediately shut her laptop.

The morning started off relatively busy, with several customers, including some needing help with rare finds. A tap on her shoulder made Simone squeal in fright, stand and spin, her heart rate propelling her upward.

'Gah!'

The figure behind her was dressed in a black fedora, a red bow tie and thick-rimmed glasses.

'Are you trying to scare me to death?'

'Sorry. I was trying to be inconspicuous.'

'Looking like that?'

'I dialled 1-800-Disguise.'

'Seriously?'

'Seriously. You can get anything delivered these days. I've decided to help you out.'

'Ed…'

'It'll be fine. I need something to do. I need distracting. There were no emails waiting for me this morning. The video meetings I had today were cancelled.'

'Oh, Ed.' She didn't know what that meant but it didn't sound good.

'I'm sure there's some other explanation. The government's busy…'

Ed frowned. Something was happening in Florena's inner government circles and its trade envoy to North America was clearly not supposed to know what it was.

'There must be things you need to do. Away from the counter. Away from the bookshop, even.'

There were. She needed to shelve the new books and take some online orders to the post office, and she had no idea when she was going to manage to do that. André was due for a shift later that afternoon, but in the meantime she was alone.

'There are—thank you. I do need to go to the post office.'

'Go out for an hour or so. I'll be fine.'

'What if you're recognised?'

'Firstly, the further I am from Florena the less recognised I am. Secondly, who is going to believe that the silly man in the fake glasses and the bow tie in a Paris bookshop is me?'

'*I* don't believe the silly man in the fake glasses and the bow tie in a Paris bookshop is you.'

'See? I've fooled you, and you know me better than anyone in the world.'

His words made her heart pause. Even after all these years he still thought of her like that.

'Ed, there are plenty of people who know you. Who could recognise you.'

'It'll be fine. Besides, depending on how things go, I might need to ask you for a permanent job, and customer service experience will look good on my CV.'

Her heart broke for him. And his family. And everyone at the palace. 'It's not going to come to that.'

'There's no need for a crown prince of Florena, or even a trade envoy from Florena, if Florena doesn't exist.'

'Ed…' She slid her hand up his arm and squeezed his shoulder, but stopped just short of pulling him into a full embrace. Feeling the warmth of his body under her fingertips, she felt her heart get caught in her throat. She finally managed to say, 'Your father will take care of it. The Florenans won't stand for it. There are so many things standing in Laurent's way.'

He scoffed and she sighed. She wasn't going to be able to convince him. But he was right about one thing. He needed to be doing something other than watching the news and spiralling into despair.

'I need to go to the post office. If anyone wants something in particular that you can't find, take their details and I'll get back to them.'

'I can do this, Simone.'

This time he touched her arm. It was only to reassure her, but it felt as though he'd kissed her.

Kissed? Your heart rate couldn't handle it if he kissed you.

She gave him a quick explanation of the payment machine and gathered the parcels. As she walked along the street, dodging the tourists and breathing in the crisp autumn air, she was glad to have some space, but couldn't shake him completely from her thoughts.

Something was different about him. The casual comments. On their own they were nothing, but they were adding up.

'You're a goddess.'

'You know me better than anyone else.'

'What if I can't keep my hands off you?'

What was going on with him? He'd never been flirty like this with her before.

But the last time they'd spent this much time alone together they had been kids.

They'd seen each other since childhood, but usually there had been others around. Her mother or palace staff. They emailed one another occasionally. And he'd send her the occasional text message, usually to show her where he was in the world. Those messages would delight her and break her heart just a little as well. They only highlighted how their lives were on different paths.

This was different.

He was different.

He's stressed. He's going through a crisis and you're his oldest friend. He is relying on you and only you. He's just grateful and appreciates your friendship. That's all.

Once she'd posted the parcels and her hands were free Simone dialled her mother's number and was relieved when Alea picked up straight away.

'Darling. How are things? Did you see the press conference?'

'We did.'

'What a mess! How's Eddie?'

Simone smiled at her mother's use of her old name for him. 'Stressed.'

'Of course he is. But there's nowhere better for him to be right now.'

'He really wants to go home. I'm not sure how much longer he'll last here.'

'I honestly don't know what the King's long game is. There are rumours, but…'

'What sort of rumours?'

'Oh, just silly rumours. I'm sure things will quieten down soon.'

'Rumours about the Queen? Do you really think they'll divorce?'

'I don't see how it could be otherwise, to be honest.'

Simone stopped walking in the middle of the street, to the annoyance of the couple walking behind her. She stepped into a doorway.

'Ed hasn't even heard from his mother yet. I suppose that makes sense.'

'Don't say anything to Ed. As I said, we don't really know.'

Simone doubted she'd be telling Ed anything he hadn't already thought of. A royal divorce, a royal wedding and a royal baby seemed to all loom on the horizon.

Poor Ed. Having your parents' marriage disintegrate was bad, no matter how old you were. And having to go through it in the spotlight was even worse.

'I'd better get back to him. Let me know if you hear anything at all.'

'Of course. You too. Mwah.' Her mother blew her a kiss and ended the call.

Simone looked up at the great sky. Autumn was coming to its end and she could feel the change in the air.

Ed had spent the morning in the bookshop. He wasn't sure if he was helping or making a nuisance of himself, but it was better than staring at his phone or the four walls of Simone's apartment. Being in the bookshop, spending time with Simone, helped keep his mind off other things. When he was near Simone it felt as though everything would be all right. Somehow.

Around midday Simone went out to pick up some baguettes for lunch, and after that Ed went upstairs, to see if anyone had sent him any work. They hadn't. And the video conferences scheduled for the next day had disappeared from his calendar.

He groaned. He hated feeling useless.

The King didn't answer, but Ed was no longer surprised. He tried his father's secretary, who told him the King was in a meeting and would call as soon as he could. The King should change his voicemail message to say that and spare everyone the time.

He was used to this distance between him and his father, but still found it ridiculous that they had to communicate through a third person. If Ed ever had children they would always be able to reach him, whenever they wanted.

Not that he was going to have children. He'd told his parents as much. It was the one royal duty they couldn't ask of him. He'd do the job, but he wouldn't subject any woman to life in the fishbowl that was the palace of Villenueve. His parents had looked at one another, but not argued. How could they? They knew they were the very reason their son would never walk down the aisle.

Besides, his cousins had children, and now he was going to have a younger sibling the royal succession was hardly in danger.

Ed had no intention of marrying so he would not have children. He was always very careful about that. Unlike his father, he thought bitterly.

Besides, living a single life wasn't a problem. He'd never found someone he knew he could trust enough. Or someone he wanted to spend time with when the initial rush of seduction had worn off. He'd never been obsessed by a woman. Never been ready to chuck in his whole life for her.

Ed tried to read some reports but unsurprisingly he couldn't concentrate. He stretched and attempted some sit-ups and push-ups, the only exercise possible in the tiny apartment, though that too failed to clear his head.

What would happen to him if Laurent got his way? Presumably, his family would have to leave the palace. But could he still live in Florena or would he be an exile? He could come to Paris. Find a place—a bigger place, near to Simone. He could see her every day. They could be neighbours just like they'd used to be.

His body relaxed instantly at the thought. If Simone were fully in his life again he would be able to cope with whatever came next. The realisation was both surprising and comforting.

Would it be the end of the world to be an ordinary person? He knew other princes and princesses often longed to shake off their titles, but he never had. Apart from playing a few childhood games, he had never wanted to be anyone else.

Childhood games. The memories made him smile. Once upon a time, when they were very young, he and Simone had loved to play make-believe. They just hadn't always agreed on what to pretend to be.

'I want to play kings and queens,' she'd say.

He'd groan. 'But that's not pretending.'

'You're not King. I'm not Queen. It's still make-believe.'

'Detectives.'

'We always play that.'

'Okay, you can be a princess and I'll be a superhero.'

'I want to be a superhero too. A superhero princess.'

Simone had pretended to be a princess disguised as a superhero and they had run around the garden chasing Suzette, who had apparently robbed several banks.

He smiled. He'd have to remind her of that tonight.

But if he wasn't a prince he wasn't going to be a superhero either. Who would he be? Plain old Ed Berringer, former prince?

No. Laurent was not going to get his way. Abolishing Florena was inconceivable.

Tomorrow the news cycle will have moved on and I can go home. Everyone will forget what Laurent was saying and get on with their lives.

Yeah, that's what you thought yesterday.

Ed walked over to the bookshelf. Only a special kind of person would have two storeys of books downstairs and then have another bookshelf in their shoebox apartment. He glanced at the titles, but his eyes were drawn to the shelf with a collection of framed photographs. He picked up one that looked as though it had been taken on a night out or at a party.

Simone wore a strappy red dress, not unlike the one in that video. She wasn't looking at the camera, but at the man next to her. Her smile was magical, uninhibited. Ed felt as though he'd been punched in the stomach and put the frame down as if it was on fire.

The woman in the photograph—the woman downstairs—was beautiful. Grown up, sophisticated, self-assured.

He sighed. If his family were kicked out of Florena, living in Paris, being near Simone, would have its benefits.

He should stop moping and do some work. He was still the trade envoy to North America—for the time being at least.

CHAPTER SEVEN

ED WAS WAITING when she got to the top of the stairs. He was wearing the fedora and the silly glasses. 'Do you have dinner plans?' he asked.

'I thought we could order something in,' Simone replied.

'How about ordering something out?'

'Go out? But, Ed…'

'Not to a restaurant…maybe just have a walk. It's dark. We can go along the quieter streets.'

Her heart leapt. She'd love to go out with Ed, and could tell he was bursting to leave the apartment.

'Are you sure?'

'If you can bear to be seen with me?'

He did look slightly ridiculous. In addition to the hat, glasses and bow tie, he'd found an old black coat of hers.

'In that get-up? I wouldn't miss it.'

He smiled.

Simone bought a bottle of Burgundy with a screw top from the shop across the road and they picked up a box of pizza from her favourite place down the street. They made their way to the Seine. The light had gone and they found a section of the bank with no one around and sat, with their legs dangling over the edge, taking turns to drink the wine straight out of the bottle.

Ed seemed relaxed, but Simone kept looking around.

'Relax. There's no one. I have a sixth sense for photographers. Besides, we look like students down here, with our wine in a brown paper bag.'

'I am surprised you came to me,' she confessed, taking a sip of the wine.

'I was in Paris. You're my person in Paris.'

Of course. That was all. She was convenient. The nearest warm body.

'I was just wondering…' The wine had loosened her tongue. But he'd probably be gone in the morning, so she might as well ask her question now. 'Are they pressuring you at all?'

'What about?'

'To find someone. Get married. Produce an heir and all that.'

Her mouth was dry when she asked. She'd never been quite so direct with him. They talked about other things, not relationships.

'Always.'

'Is there someone?'

'Are you asking if I'm dating someone?'

'Well, I suppose so. Yes.'

He laughed. 'No, Sim. I'm not dating anyone. I would've told you long before this if I was.'

He leant towards her, close enough that she could see the crinkles around his eyes through his fake glasses when he smiled, and said, 'Simone, I'd always tell you something like that.'

'You would?'

'You're my person.'

'Your person *in Paris*,' she clarified.

'No. My person. Full stop.'

The muscles in her chest tightened. 'Really?'

'Yes.'

Despite the cool air, her face was warm. His eyes were too serious. She closed the lid to the pizza box and brushed invisible crumbs from her lap.

He just means you're his friend—that's all. You've always known that. It's not a surprise.

But the way her heart was beating so fast at his declaration was a surprise.

They were best friends. It should be enough. But one day Ed would marry a beautiful princess. Or a movie star. And Simone would be back to being his person in Paris.

'But if they're pressuring you? Your parents?'

'They've been throwing heiresses in my direction for the past decade.'

'And?'

'I keep ignoring them. Delaying. It's not something I plan on doing. I told you this, didn't I?'

'Yes, when you were twelve.'

'It's still the plan.'

She'd never have to stand in the royal cathedral in Florena and watch him get married to someone else. It was something at least.

'But what about the monarchy. Having an heir?'

'Not you too!' He pushed himself back, making to stand.

'No. I don't care. Honestly.' That was a big fat lie. This was one of the most significant conversations she'd had in years. 'I'm just curious. Your parents must have said something?'

'Yeah, well, I try to avoid their questions. It only leads to arguments. But now that I'm going to have a sibling it's worked out great. I'm about to have a younger brother or sister. They can inherit after me. As far as I'm concerned it's the one good thing to come out of this mess. They'll have to stop hassling me for an heir. Father's done that for me.'

'You can't be serious?'

'Why can't I be?'

They sat in silence, watching the lights reflecting in the river and the boats slowly passing by.

After a while she couldn't help herself. 'Can I ask why? As a disinterested bystander not as your parent.'

He looked at her again, his eyes narrowed in sharp focus. That look of his made something inside her flip.

'Sorry. It's personal. You don't have to tell me,' she said quickly.

'I'm happy to tell you. It's not a secret.'

She held her breath.

'I'm a playboy looking for the nearest warm body. Everyone knows that.'

Something inside her twisted. 'But that's not true. Not really.'

'It's what the tabloids say.'

'But…it's all exaggeration? Lies to sell papers?' She held her breath, and her heart seemed to stop as she waited for his answer. She knew Ed's reputation, but she also knew Ed. He wasn't a womaniser. Or was he?

'Yes, it's lies…mostly. But…'

'But what?' Simone felt sick, waiting for his answer. What wasn't he telling her? Had he really slept with half the models in Europe?

'I don't think I have what it takes. Besides, I don't believe that love lasts. Certainly not long enough to sustain a long marriage. If anything, the events of this week just prove it. My parents hate one another. They've made one another miserable. Mine wasn't a happy childhood home. You know that.'

It had been barely a home. Ed's parents had often been away, and when they'd been around, Ed had just seemed unhappier.

'But not every couple is like that. My parents were happy.'

He looked as though he were considering his next words carefully. 'Everyone falls out of love eventually.'

Her heart cracked. If only that were the case…

'You didn't know my parents together,' she said. 'Did *you*, though?'

He probably meant that she must have only vague

memories of her parents together, but you only had to see how Alea still spoke about her husband to know that love could last years and years—even beyond death.

'Your parents might be unhappy. That doesn't mean every couple is. Have you ever been in love?' The question was out before she realised she didn't actually want to know the answer.

'No.'

She exhaled. Of course he hadn't been in love. If he'd really felt the exquisite pull and pain of true love he wouldn't be saying this.

'Have you?' he asked.

If her face hadn't been red before, by now it would be setting off fire alarms.

She looked at her plate and considered her answer.

'That's a yes,' he said.

'I didn't say that.'

'It's a yes—otherwise you wouldn't look like that.'

'Like what?' she squawked.

'Like you don't want to answer the question. And it ended badly, didn't it?'

It didn't even begin.

She pressed her fingers to her burning cheeks to cool them.

Ed raised an eyebrow, but he must have noticed her discomfort because he didn't ask anything further.

They watched the boats a while longer, and when they had finished the wine Ed stood and offered

Simone his hand to help her stand. She took it hesitantly, anticipating the jolt that would race through her. Yep—there it was. As predictable and inconvenient as ever.

They walked along the bank, up the river and then climbed the stone stairs to cross the Pont d'Austerlitz.

Halfway along Ed stopped.

The middle of a Parisian bridge looking up the Seine must surely be one of the most romantic places on the planet. Why was he doing this to her?

Ed turned his face to the sky, giving her a moment to steal a glance at his beautiful torso and then his face. Free to study him, she let her gaze follow the line of his strong jawbone, move over his cheekbones and rest on his soft brown eyelashes. Even in the silly glasses he was still heart-stopping.

'Have you been in touch with your mother?' he asked.

'Yes. She doesn't know much.'

'Has she seen my father?'

'Apparently no one has apart from his private secretary. And Laurent.'

'Laurent's been at the palace?'

Simone nodded. 'At least once a day, apparently.'

'Checking the joint out?'

'Meeting with your father, they say.'

'Did she say what the mood's like?'

'Tense. Sad.'

She didn't want to tell him everything her mother had said. It would just make him worry. Everyone was very concerned about their jobs, about Florena, but also about the royal family.

'Mum knows you're here. I couldn't lie to her. But she hasn't told anyone except to let them know you're somewhere safe and loving.'

Loving? She couldn't believe that word had come out of her mouth. It was the word her mother had used, but Simone hadn't expected to repeat it.

Ed studied her through narrowed eyes. It was that new, strange look she had seen a bit lately. As if he was puzzled by her.

Great.

He wasn't attracted to her. He was puzzled. It was a step up from 'I think of you as a friend', at least.

'Do you remember we used to play pretend?' he asked.

'Of course. Detectives and superheroes.'

'You always wanted to play kings and queens.'

'Yeah, but we had to play superheroes because you said, "Kings and queens isn't pretending." Even though I was definitely not a queen. And we had a palace to pretend in and everything. But no, we had to investigate who had taken Suzette's dog toys. I knew all along that you had hidden them.'

Ed laughed. 'I'd forgotten that.' He looked thoughtful for a moment. His green soulful eyes stared, unfocused, over the water.

'We did play kings and queens once.'

A memory long forgotten, dreamlike, surfaced into her consciousness. They'd been in the palace, had sneaked into the throne room one evening when his parents had been away and the staff distracted. Ed, who'd felt comfortable in the room, had run around with Suzette. Simone, who had not shared his ease at being in the throne room, had entered the room carefully and with awe. It was lined with gilded mirrors and portraits of past kings and queens of Florena, and they had looked down at them with disapproval as Ed had chased the dog until she barked.

Her chest warmed—as much from the memory as from the fact that he had remembered.

No one knew her like he did.

'You told me to sit on the throne,' she said.

'And I crowned you with my baseball hat.'

She laughed. 'Why?'

'Because you wanted to be crowned and that was all we had.'

'I was eight. I probably did.'

The baseball hat had felt precious and serious while they were pretending. Now she shuddered. A crown would be an impossible weight to bear.

Which was fine, since Ed was never getting married and didn't believe in love. And since she was never going to return to Florena.

A boat full of drunken revellers passed underneath them. They were waving, as boat passengers often did. Ed waved back and she laughed.

'What if they recognise you?'

'In my brilliant disguise?'

'Even in that. Those glasses are ridiculous.'

She reached for them, as if to pull them off, but her hand froze. Ed's hand had wrapped around hers, preventing her revealing his disguise to the world. He was meant to be incognito. But she wanted to see his face without them.

They were so close. She knew she should let go, but it was like trying to separate magnets. He pulled her hand away from his glasses, but far from letting it go he drew their clasped hands into his chest.

They mustn't be seen. It would be bad if he were recognised—worse if she were seen with him. But still she was stuck. Ed didn't let her go and she didn't pull herself free.

She could hardly breathe. Tonight the rest of the world had fallen away. Tonight the only thing stopping her standing on her toes and kissing him was the wall she had built around her heart. And that wall was starting to feel less like stone and more like paper.

Thin tissue paper.

That could be blown away with the merest breeze.

Like the air that escaped Ed's lips as he sighed. 'Simone...'

He didn't sound hesitant. He sounded tortured. He sounded like her heart felt.

Just as she was about to step back his lips were on hers. It was quick. Even though Simone had been thinking of kissing Ed, the surprise nearly brought her knees out from under her. It might also have been the perfect way Ed's lips fitted against hers. The way his fingers tilted her head to the precise angle needed to send blissful sparks shooting through her.

She pulled herself back. What was he thinking? This was madness.

'I'm sorry… I thought you wanted… I misread.' He looked at the ground.

This was ridiculous. He wasn't to blame any more than she was.

'No, you didn't misread.'

He lifted his gaze back to hers. Through the clear lenses of the glasses she could feel the gravity in his next question. 'You wanted to kiss me?'

'Want. Present tense.'

She lifted herself up onto her toes, feeling his body rub against hers as she brought her lips to his mouth.

The sensation of his hard body pressing against hers only blew that wall further into oblivion. Had she gone too far? Would they be seen? No. They wouldn't be identified out of all the other couples making out on all of Paris's beautiful bridges.

His broad hands slid up her back and into her hair. He gently held her head in place while he covered her with kisses. From her lips to her neck. Behind her ears and back again.

Ed is kissing you. His tongue is currently in your mouth. You can feel him. All of him. What does it mean? He doesn't believe in love, so what is this?

She ordered the voices in her head that were telling her to be careful to stop. Not to ruin what could be the most perfect moment of her life. She wanted to live in the moment. Savour each kiss, each caress, each heartbeat.

His tongue, tasting of red wine and hope, slid past hers. His muscles slackened and then tensed under her hands, which for the first time had the freedom to roam where they wanted to over Ed. She slid one hand over his shoulders, around the soft nape of his neck into his thick hair.

It was something she'd only dreamt of. The feel of his skin. The taste of his mouth. She'd rehearsed it in her head so often as a teenager, but the sensations coasting through her body still caught her off guard. There was no way she could have prepared herself for the way her muscles shivered when he slid his hand down her back, rested it on her bottom and pulled her firmly against him.

When the desire pooling inside her was about to overflow, the voice of reason became louder and she pulled her mouth back from his. She caught her breath and saw he was doing the same.

His face was flushed and his breath shallow, and it took every last ounce of her sanity to ask, 'What's going on?'

CHAPTER EIGHT

SHE EXHALED WITH a half-sigh, half-groan, and Ed trembled as he answered.

'I don't know. Maybe we could make it up as we go along.'

His lips travelled past her ear, down her neck to the low neckline of her dress and she wobbled on her stilettos. He held her tight and steadied her. He checked that she was all right, then he closed his eyes and kissed her again.

'Is that okay?' he murmured into her neck.

There was no roadmap where he was going. This was uncharted territory. Off-road into the unknown.

But what if he got hopelessly lost?

You're already lost. You may as well see where this leads.

This was a far better way to be spending his time than fretting about his future. Simone's kisses were sweet and soft, and after trying just one he was completely, hopelessly addicted.

That's probably why you never kissed her before. You knew it would be impossible to stop.

'Are you sure this is a good idea?' she asked.

He couldn't remember being more certain of anything. Kissing her. Wanting her. It was like gravity. The sun, the moon and the tides.

There were probably good reasons why they shouldn't be doing this, but with Simone in his arms they paled into insignificance.

'For starters we're friends,' she said.

That was the very reason he wanted to kiss her and slip this dress off her gorgeous body. To feel every inch of her. Because she was Simone. His oldest friend. His beautiful, amazing friend.

He guessed that must be what she meant. Friends sometimes didn't want to sleep together because they were afraid it would ruin their friendship. The thought hadn't occurred to him. This would only deepen their relationship. Make it even more special.

'Our friendship won't change. It's too old for that and too strong.'

He layered kisses along her low neckline, nudging the fabric down even further as he went. Maybe she did have a point. If he lowered his mouth much further maybe everything would change between them. The taste of her skin and the warmth of her pressed against him caused another thought. Their relationship might change, but only for the better. He'd never felt so close to her. That had to be a good thing, didn't it?

He'd never slept with his best friend before. He'd never slept with a friend before. So how did he really know?

You know that Simone will always be in your life. You know that losing her isn't an option.

He felt her body lean into him, her desire matching his, letting him know she agreed. The skin of her hand was unspeakably soft. He had to keep going back over it with his fingertip to see if it really was as beautiful as if felt. Soft and warm. Alive.

'But not here,' she said, thankfully being sensible enough for both of them.

It was dangerous enough for him to be out and about, let alone losing himself like this in public.

He wanted her. All of her. And it was threatening to overwhelm everything else.

He grabbed her hand and pulled her in the direction of her apartment. They walked fast, but each time they had to stop to cross a road they would kiss again, and inevitably fall back into the kisses. He wanted to get back to the apartment, but he was enjoying the lingering and anticipation nearly as much.

They stopped to kiss on every street. They stopped to kiss in front of the bookshop. On the stairs, on the landing. And finally they were inside her apartment, jackets being pulled off and shoes kicked away.

He trailed kisses along her collarbone and felt her shiver.

Then a buzzing startled them both, and Simone's limbs froze beneath his hands.

'Is that your phone?'

Leave it, he was about to say. But he knew it was hopeless. He couldn't give his whole self to her while he wondered what the call was about. Who it was.

'Check it. You have to check it.' Simone untangled herself from him.

He wasn't sure if his decision to leave his phone behind had been accidental or deliberate, but it had been serendipitous. Because there were many missed calls.

Calls that would have disrupted his evening with Simone.

Calls that he needed to return.

'My father,' he said.

'Should I leave you?'

'No. Stay. Please.'

Ed didn't bother listening to the messages. He wanted the news straight from his father. He sat on the couch and motioned for Simone to sit next to him.

He dialled his father and placed the phone on speaker. Simone's eyes widened, but he simply picked up her hand and squeezed it.

'Ed. You took your time.'

'Sorry, Father. I was caught up.' Ed squeezed Simone's hand again and she squeezed back.

'I've made a decision. It is mine alone to make. I've abdicated the throne. I signed the papers just over an hour ago.'

'You're abdicating?' The words felt strange on his tongue.

'I have already—Your Majesty.'

It sounded like a joke. A cruel, cruel joke. Made all the worse by the timing. He could hardly bear to look at Simone, sitting next to him. She rested her head on his shoulder.

'There should be a car arriving for you shortly. It will take you straight to the airport. We can talk more when you get here. I'm about to speak to the press.'

Ed couldn't answer—not even to argue. He knew, as well as his father did, that there was no point. It was done.

His father ended the call.

Don't make any decisions without me.

Ed wanted to throw up. He was now the King of Florena. King Edouard the Fourth of Florena.

He focused on his breathing, hoping the news would start to sink in if he did.

Another day, another night, and they might have a chance to figure out what was happening between them.

'That's all? It's done?'

Simone was as shocked as he was at the swiftness of the King's actions. At the brevity of the phone call.

Ed laughed. 'He didn't even ask how I was.'

'You're not even there. He didn't wait for you to get back.'

'That's been the point all along.' He could taste the bitterness in his voice. 'That's why I had to stay—so that I wouldn't be standing next to him now. So that I wouldn't talk him out of it. So that I wouldn't have a choice.'

She nodded. 'He should have talked to you. Should've involved you.'

'But that would have been too hard for him. Over these past few days my father's hardly proved himself to be a man of courage or honour.'

Simone stood to get them both a drink. She pulled a dusty bottle of Scotch down from her top cupboard and poured them both generous glasses. Then she turned on the small television and they waited. The tickertape announced that the King of Florena would be giving a live address at any moment.

Ed wondered how long they had before the knock at the door came and he was taken away.

The screen changed to a shot of the palace of Villeneuve and then to the King.

Except he's not the King any more. You are.

His father looked tired as he sat behind a desk and looked down the camera.

'Thank you all for joining me this evening. It has become apparent over the past few days that I am not the best person to be serving this country. I have allowed my personal life to distract me from my duties and I have not been the King you deserve or the man I want to be.'

The Scotch burnt Ed's throat on the way down, but he still took another large sip.

'The most appropriate person to be serving our beautiful country is my son, Edouard, who as of one hour ago became your sovereign. Edouard is devoted to this country, and I know he will dedicate his entire life to your service.'

'He was talking about you like you aren't a real person,' Simone whispered, once the King had finished.

'But from now on I'm not. Not really. I'm the sovereign. The head of state. The embodiment of Florena.'

He had to go back to Florena and save his country.

Simone clenched her fists and paced the room. It only took four steps in each direction, so she was pretty much going in circles.

How would he get through the next few days without her? How would he get through the nights? Less than half an hour ago they'd been undressing one another. Now…? Now he was lost.

'Come with me.'

If he couldn't stay, she could come.

She shook her head and kept shaking it. As if she was convincing herself it was the right decision.

He knew what she should do. 'You could come with me—please.'

'I can't leave the bookshop.'

'I'll pay for someone to look after the bookshop. Please.'

'Oh, no, no, no. That's not how things are going to work.'

'What do you mean?'

'I mean… I just can't.'

'Is it about the money?'

'It's the whole damn thing! Ed, this is happening so fast.'

She didn't need to tell *him* that. He'd been the monarch for ninety minutes and hadn't even known for most of that time.

He needed her. Couldn't imagine going back to Florena and getting through the next period without her. He didn't want to return without her by his side.

The realisation was almost as overwhelming as the news his father had just delivered.

He wanted Simone.

He needed her. As he needed air.

What had happened between them on the bridge hadn't been an aberration.

'Come with me. Please.'

He stood and went to her, grasping her shoulders with his hands and stopping her pacing.

She looked up at him, but her expression was pained. 'Ed... What would I be?'

'What do you mean?'

'You know what I mean. If I came with you, what would I be?'

Ah, right...

Why couldn't they just be Simone and Ed? Best friends? Surely not everything had to change at once.

'You would be my friend.'

She grimaced. 'And I'd just sit in the palace all day as your *friend*?'

Would that be so bad? She was his best friend,

and now they were exploring whether she might be something more.

She looked at him, as if waiting for him to catch up. Would she be his *girlfriend*? Did kings even *have* girlfriends? He knew the answer to that. Kings had wives. And they had mistresses. And Simone would be neither his wife nor his mistress.

Bringing a new, unsteady relationship into the mix at this point would make things in Florena go from bad to worse. There was no room for exploring their new relationship now he was the new king. There was no room for missteps, break-ups, gossip or rumours. There was no room for them to see how this new side of their relationship developed naturally. Privately.

She was ten steps ahead of him. She'd already seen the problems that he wanted to ignore.

'The absolute last thing you need is gossip and speculation about your personal life,' she told him.

'I see what you mean. It's complicated.'

But how was he going to get through this without her?

Simone couldn't be more than his best friend because he didn't believe in love. And throwing a nascent relationship into the mess that was the current saga of the Florenan royal family...

He couldn't do that to her. And he couldn't do it to his people.

His people.

'Ed, I want to be with you. Please know that. You

are one of the most important people in the world to me. And I want to help you. But do you really think me going with you…as things are now…is that the best thing for Florena? For you?'

He picked up her hand and turned it over in his, steadying his breath and his thoughts. Her skin was soft. Her nails short and clean. He wanted to know these hands as well as he knew his own.

Damn, why could he taste salt in the back of his nose?

Because you're going to miss her. Because standing up and walking out of this room is going to be the hardest thing you've done in your life.

He looked at her and almost broke—but didn't. He wasn't being fair on Simone. It wouldn't be fair to drag her into the circus of which he was now the ringmaster.

This is what you always knew, isn't it?

It wouldn't be fair to subject a woman to the scrutiny of the Florenan royal family. He couldn't do it to anyone he really cared about. Least of all Simone.

He choked out a rueful laugh. It was either that or cry.

'Is there nothing I can say to make you come with me?' he asked, though he already knew the answer.

'You know as well as I do that having me there will just make it worse for you. And my life is here. I can't just abandon it for a few months.'

'A few months?'

'Well, yes… Until you find your feet. Until…'

She didn't need to finish the sentence. *Until we break up.*

Because he didn't believe in love. Or marriage.

He looked back down at her hands, still wrapped around his. Keeping him anchored. He was afraid to let them go. Afraid that when he did she would float away from him.

There was nothing else to do but say goodbye.

He cupped her chin in his palm and tilted her mouth towards his. He opened his mouth and pulled her in, making sure that every taste, every shiver, every sigh was marked indelibly onto his memory. But as he did so he felt his eyes fill with water.

He pulled back and saw his own tears glistening on her cheeks. He brushed one away with the back of his thumb. She jumped back as though she'd been scolded.

'Goodbye,' she squeaked, before pulling away and moving to the door. 'Good luck.'

She grabbed her coat and closed the door behind her before he could catch his breath to reply.

CHAPTER NINE

THE ENGRAVED INVITATION arrived for her just before Christmas.

> *The presence of*
> *Simone Auclair*
> *is requested*
> *at the coronation of*
> *King Edouard the Fourth of Florena*
> *on 31st January at 11 a.m.*
> *Dress: full morning dress.*
> *The coronation will be followed by*
> *a state dinner and ball.*
> *Further instructions will be provided upon your*
> *acceptance of this invitation.*

With the invitation, or summons—she wasn't sure which—was a handwritten note.

> *Dearest Sim,*
> *I know it might be hard for you to come back to Florena, but I can't imagine getting through this day without my best friend.*
> *All my love, Ed.*

She turned the card over and slipped it under a book on her desk. Go back to Florena? Not just for a quick flying visit to her mother but to go to the coronation? And a ball? To be seen and photographed?

You don't have to go.

It was true. No one would tie her up and force her to attend. And once the coronation was over she would be free to leave.

She didn't have a choice. Not really.

I can't imagine getting through this day without my best friend.

My best friend. After everything, he was still her best friend, and this was probably the most important day of his life. As hard as it would be for her, it would be unforgivable not to be there for him.

To go as his friend.

He'd said that on that wonderful and horrible evening two months ago, before he'd been whisked away to assume his duties. He might as well have asked her to go as his sister.

'Friend' was something, though. It wasn't nothing.

But even after their kisses he was still thinking of her as just his friend.

That time on the bridge had nearly ripped her in two. There was no doubt in her mind that if the phone call from his father had come later they would have made love and their relationship would have changed for ever.

She sighed. It didn't matter what either of them had thought or felt on the bridge that night.

She couldn't have gone to Florena as anything

but his friend. Now that he was King there was really no possibility of them being together. Friendship would be all they were allowed to have. No matter how much their bodies might wish otherwise. Ed knew that. Her heart just had to realise too.

To be fair to Ed, he hadn't meant to hurt her or insult her by asking her to go to Florena as his friend. He really did want his friend there by his side. And she wanted to be there for him too—as his friend, apart from anything else.

She ached when she thought of him in Florena on his own, facing his new life. Alone.

Once it's over you will leave.

CHAPTER TEN

SIMONE HADN'T BEEN back to Florena for over two years. Her mother always joined her in Paris for a week over Christmas, so Simone did not have to leave the bookshop. It had been a decade since Simone had called the kingdom home, and now she could see the country as any visitor might.

The palace sat on a high peak, keeping watch over the city and the great valley of Florena. In summer the valley was green and lush. Now, in midwinter, the slopes were covered in their famous powdery snow.

The small country was picturesque.

Her heart began to soar when she saw it, but she caught it and pushed it back down again. Florena might look as if it had been ripped from the pages of a fairy tale, but she knew better. She knew that looks were deceiving and fairy tales were most definitely not real.

The apartment where Simone had grown up was two storeys above the palace kitchen. The building was nearly as old as the main palace, but in the last century the upper levels had been converted into comfortable and spacious apartments for the senior staff.

Their living room overlooked the ancient cobblestoned courtyard that palace staff criss-crossed all day, going about their lives much as they had for centuries. Doing laundry, gardening and cooking.

Simone's old bedroom had a view of one of the palace's private walled gardens. The manicured grass where Ed and Simone had once played with Suzette was now covered in snow.

She was privileged to have grown up there and to be able to return when she wanted to visit Alea, who had now been given the security of a lifetime tenancy in her apartment—one of the last things the former King had done before abdicating.

The old King Edouard might have deeply hurt his son in the way he'd abandoned the crown without consultation, but Simone could not help being grateful for the way he'd thought about his loyal staff at the end—especially with everything else on his mind.

Simone understood that the King—that was the former King, now styled as the Duke of Armiel—was living in southern France with Celine, awaiting the birth of their daughter in the coming May.

The Queen, who still held that title, had only returned to Florena briefly and quietly, and was now dividing her time between the Caribbean and New York. She had agreed to a divorce, but the negotiations over property were fraught. Simone understood from her mother and from general rumour that the Queen would keep half her fortune, leaving the remaining half with Ed. Ed had some money his maternal grandfather had left directly to him, but the Queen's fortune was so large that even half of it still left both of them on most rich lists. The new Duke of Armiel would have to rely on his own funds, which were believed to be small, along with generosity from Ed.

Ed… She sighed.

He had been in touch since he'd left Paris, with occasional messages and phone calls that were memorable for all the wrong reasons. There'd been either long pauses or they'd spoken over one another. Even their messages had been polite and perfunctory. Neither of them had dared to mention that night in Paris.

The morning after her arrival back in the palace, Simone sat looking out of the window at the activity in the courtyard with a cup of hot coffee warming her hands.

'What are you doing today?' her mother asked as she ate her breakfast.

'Relaxing here, I think.'

'Do you have plans to see Ed?'

Simone shook her head. Ed knew Simone had accepted her invitation to the coronation, but she hadn't told him exactly when she would arrive. He'd be busy with preparations and with being King. He wouldn't have time for her.

'I think he'd like to see you. He'd appreciate seeing a friendly face.'

Simone wanted to pump her mother for further information, but didn't want to risk giving anything away. She wasn't even mentally prepared to answer questions about Ed, let alone to see him.

They'd kissed. Made out as they'd wound their way across Paris like teenagers or tourists. And if that phone call hadn't come from Ed's father they would, she was ninety-nine per cent sure, have ended up in bed. Any reservations she might have had had been shattered as he'd held her and she'd felt how much he'd wanted her too.

'Never mind,' her mother said. 'Do you have an outfit for the coronation?'

Simone nodded. 'An advantage of living in Paris.'

She'd spent some of her precious savings on it, but she was determined to look amazing.

'And for the ball?'

'I don't think I'll go.'

'What? You must come. All the long-standing staff have been invited.'

Simone winced. She knew she couldn't miss the coronation…but the ball? It was a social event and she would feel completely out of place. Besides, her mother's comment confirmed what Simone had expected. All the long-term staff of the palace were invited. Simone's invitation was by virtue of her mother's position only.

'So I take it you don't have a dress?'

'No. So, you see, I can't go.' She shrugged.

'Not so fast, *mademoiselle*. I may have something… It might need taking in, but we're a similar size.'

Alea disappeared into her room and returned with a large white box. She lifted the lid and Simone gasped. The box was overflowing with raw silver silk. Her mother lifted miles of fabric out of the box, revealing a bodice with a sweetheart neckline. The bodice was embroidered with intricate flowers and swirls.

It was a work of art.

'When did you get this?'

Simone had thought she was aware of most of the formal wear in her mother's wardrobe, and was sure she would not have missed something like this.

'Oh, I'm not sure.' Alea waved the question away. 'Try it on.'

Even without make-up or her hair done, Simone was transformed. She wouldn't be inconspicuous if she wore this dress. Her plan for her stay in Florena was to fly under the radar. She wanted to avoid press attention at all costs.

'It's a statement piece,' her mother said.

'But what sort of statement would I be making?' Simone mumbled, mostly to herself.

'It says that you belong. It says you are regal.'

'But I'm not regal—and I don't think I should pretend I am.' She had no intention of pretending to be royal.

'Regal is a state of mind,' Alea said.

'I'm not sure I can back up whatever this dress is saying.'

'Why not?'

Simone shook her head. Any answer would only invite more questions.

Since arriving back in her childhood home, she had been struggling to supress her sixteen-year-old self. The naïve, uncertain parts of herself. In Paris she was confident, worldly and strong. Back here she was constantly expecting someone to remember her as the girl who had tried to serenade the Prince.

Paris, she realised, was also a state of mind. She needed to channel some of her inner Parisienne to make it through the next week.

'But you'll wear it?' her mother asked.

Simone nodded only to placate her. She would decide later if she really could subject herself to the scrutiny of a public ball.

'Great.'

Her mother kissed her and left for work, leaving Simone standing in the dress in front of the mirror. She swayed her hips and watched the fabric swirl around her legs.

Make-believe.

It wasn't real.

Just as what had happened between her and Ed wasn't real.

Oh, it had happened. She hadn't dreamt it. They had really kissed and spent an amazing evening wandering the streets of Paris together.

But her feelings were pointless, hopefully temporary, and maddening. She'd fallen for Ed once—a childhood crush, certainly, but still devastating in the way only first love could be. She wasn't going to make the mistake of falling in love with him as an adult. She'd worked too hard to overcome her heartache the first time.

And Ed's feelings for her…? They were fleeting at best. Most likely already non-existent. She'd caught Ed at a vulnerable moment. He'd been under stress because of his family problems. Trapped in her apartment. In the ordinary course of things he would never have kissed her. Much less said he wanted to sleep with her. Simone *knew* that.

Fairy tales were not real.

What *was* real were internet trolls, threats on social media and online harassment. She'd already had a taste of that, thank you very much. Now that Ed was the King, the scrutiny on anyone he dated would be intense. She wasn't up for that, emotionally or psychologically. It was part of the package Ed came with, so she needed to keep a firm lid on any feelings that threatened to rise up in her again. Like they had when she was a teenager.

So she wasn't about to drop in on him today or any other day she was here. She wasn't going to bombard him with messages that would only distract him from his duties. Or, worse, make him feel that he had to come down here and explain to her that what had happened between them in Paris had been a mistake.

Two days after the coronation she'd leave. The next time she returned to Florena would be next Christmas, and by that point the time she and Ed had spent together in Paris would be a vague memory. Something that had happened in the crazy time before the old King's abdication.

André had offered to run the bookshop while she was away and she had gratefully accepted. In the meantime, she would stay in her mother's apartment and catch up on some screen time. Watch some movies by the fire. She might help her mother out in the kitchen, but she was unlikely to cross Ed's path.

She probably wouldn't even see him. He was the King now. He'd be too busy to see her, much less anything else.

She unzipped the dress, climbed out of it, and went for a shower.

Ed hadn't thought it would be easy leaving Simone in Paris, but he hadn't expected it to be as hard as it had been. He'd walked away from women before, and even though Simone was different from the others he hadn't expected this.

Constantly looking around for her.

Starting to speak to her.

Reaching for her and always finding she wasn't there.

He hadn't expected to go to bed hoping to dream about her.

He hadn't expected to feel so devastated each time he woke to find she wasn't next to him. That he had to face another long day alone.

The past few months had been the most stressful in his life. The abdication, defending the country against pressure from Laurent and now preparing for the coronation… It had been enough to push even the most resilient person to the brink.

Was it any wonder his feelings for Simone were so confusing? She was his oldest friend, and now a woman he'd kissed and been minutes away from sleeping with. That didn't have to mean anything, did it? The dreams? Talking to her when she wasn't there? The longing that rippled through his body when he thought of her? That was all just because of the stress, wasn't it?

The one thing he knew for certain was that she was back in Florena today.

Last night, to be precise. Alea had told him she would arrive late. He'd figured she needed some time with her mother, but it was now the morning and Alea would have left for work. He couldn't wait another moment.

He'd wanted to call Simone every day, and each time had had to stop himself. Partly because hearing her voice wasn't the balm he'd hoped it would be. Only a further reminder of what was missing from his life. And also because what if she got the wrong idea and thought that his intentions towards her were more than they could be?

Because they couldn't be together. She lived in Paris, had a life there—a life she was rightly proud of—and he couldn't ask her to give that up. Besides, since his father's abdication, the very future of his country depended upon Ed staying out of the tabloids.

A relationship wasn't in itself a problem…but a break-up? A scandal? That would be just the sort of thing that would send his people to the polls and end the independence of his country.

That was not going to happen while Ed was King. He'd devoted his whole life to this country and he wasn't about to see it swallowed up to fulfil the political ambitions of Pierre Laurent. His role might be largely ceremonial, but that wasn't nothing. His job description stretched from diplomat to charity worker and many things in between. The monarchy gave Florenans pride in their country and in their history. It gave them stability.

It was a lot to put on one person's shoulders. Which was probably why sometimes—after the dreams, after he spoke to her when she wasn't there—he forgot all the reasons why they couldn't be together. Because he wanted her. It was selfish, but he needed her.

She should be here with him. She belonged here. She should be with him. Should share his bed and share his life.

Then he'd remember.

Duty. Fidelity. The future of Florena. The fact that no King Edouard had ever managed to stay faithful to his wife. The fact that one more scandal might spell the end of the entire country.

Ed drew a deep breath and knocked on Simone's apartment door.

Duty. Fidelity. Florena.

Simone threw open the door and said, 'Did you forget your key—? Ooh!'

Ed forgot all those things. At that moment he wasn't even capable of remembering his own name. Simone was wearing only a white towel, her skin still bright and glistening from a recent shower, her hair tied messily on her head.

Ooh! indeed.

He wanted to reply with a witty retort, but he'd forgotten every word he'd ever known.

'Ed, I'm sorry. I thought you were my mother.'

Ed. She'd called him by his shortened name. His nickname. She was the first person in three months not to call him 'Your Majesty' and he wanted to kiss her for it.

He wanted to kiss her for many reasons.

When he still couldn't respond, she said, 'You'd better come in, just in case anyone comes past.'

He followed her inside and as she reached behind him to close the door he caught her scent. Flowers. Summer.

'I'll just get dressed,' she said.

'No,' he said.

The first word out of his mouth since he'd walked in and his voice felt strange.

She gave him a questioning look.

'It's good to see you, Simone.'

He stepped towards her and leant down to kiss her cheek, breathing her in. The scent of her body-wash mixed with the steam from the shower and swirled around him. His knees weakened.

He felt a sweet sigh escape Simone's mouth—and that was the end of him. He pulled her into his arms, wet towel and all, and kissed her lips. Properly. Without hesitation or restraint. Picking up exactly where they had left off before the phone call telling him about the abdication had come.

She melted into the kiss. Paris came back to him in flashbacks: her smiles, her soft skin, their bodies pressed against one another's. His body remembered hers as if it had been yesterday. And hadn't it? Hadn't everything else in the world stopped when she hadn't been around?

'Ed!' she gasped as she pulled away. 'Is this…? Should…?'

'You're having trouble with your words too,' he said.

Her brow furrowed.

'Your mother's downstairs.'

'My mother's the least of our worries.'

'I'm not worried.'

And he wasn't. They were in private, and he trusted Simone with his life. For once his feelings were completely certain. He wanted her. As soon as possible.

'I am!'

He reluctantly let her go. As he stepped back her

towel dropped, exposing a beautiful bare breast and a very erect pink nipple. He grinned, and Simone pulled the towel to her. Muscles inside him that had been inert for the past few months suddenly woke up.

'They don't deserve to be covered up,' he said.

Her flushed face turned ever redder. 'I'm only here for a week,' she said.

'Do you mean, *I'm only here for a week so I shouldn't let that towel drop*? or do you mean, *I'm only here for a week so I may as well let the towel drop*?'

His throat went stone-dry as he waited for her answer. Just when he thought he might crack, the shadow of a grin appeared across her beautiful face.

'Maybe the latter?'

'Maybe?'

He stepped towards her. Ready to pull the towel away. Ready to rip his own shirt off his back as soon as she told him she was sure.

'What if someone finds out?' she said.

'I'm not cheating on anyone. We're two single consenting adults. We're not doing anything wrong.'

'I don't want to do anything that will jeopardise your job…the country.'

'It's unlikely anyone will ever find out. No one knows about Paris.'

He reached out and rubbed the back of his thumb over her bare shoulder. There was no one in the world he trusted more.

'Is that all you're worried about or is there something else? Say the word and I'll walk away now.'

She swallowed hard.

'Okay. I won't walk away. I'll leave the room while you get changed, and then I'll ask you to come and have a coffee with me and a walk around the garden. Which was, by the way, my original plan. You greeting me warm from the shower and wearing only a towel that doesn't seem to be able to stay up was a happy accident, but not part of my plan.'

She laughed, and he knew it would all be okay. Whatever happened.

In a rush she moved towards him and lifted herself to his lips. The surge of relief and emotion that ripped through him made him groan. Simone was in his arms. Warm, soft, wet. Smelling like soap and heaven. Tasting like coffee and home. Their lips pressed together. Their muscle memory from Paris knew exactly how to angle their heads to mesh their mouths perfectly.

She slipped her arms around his neck and pushed her fingers through his hair. His knees almost gave way. This woman was magnificent. Her sighs asked him for more and he was only too happy to give it. It was more wonderful and more satisfying than anything he'd felt since the last time he'd held her in his arms.

The towel dropped away again, this time to the floor. Simone was utterly naked, utterly gorgeous, and utterly in his arms. Suddenly his own clothing was too hot and way too tight. He shrugged off his jacket and it landed with her towel. Simone's pretty fingers dug his shirt out of his waistband and the sensation of her fingertips stroking his stomach made every muscle south of his waist tighten. She kissed him passionately as she undid his shirt buttons, one by one. He wanted to help, but his fingers were currently busy trailing their way down the smooth skin of her back to her perfect bottom.

It was a dilemma. Every second he spent undressing himself was a second he couldn't hold Simone, and he was quite sure he never wanted to let her go.

She tugged his shirt away from his body and threw it to the floor with a force that suggested she was as pleased as he was to see it gone.

Skin on skin was magical. The feeling of her bare body against his brought every sensation in his body to the surface.

'You have no idea how much I've missed you,' he murmured against her neck.

'I have some idea.'

'I've thought of you every hour… I've missed you every minute…'

Simone pulled back and looked at him. Her expression was dumbstruck. Her eyes were open wide and her jaw slack. He'd said too much and was in danger of saying even more. He didn't know how he felt about Simone. His feelings were confusing.

Overwhelming. He didn't know how to describe them to himself, let alone how to explain them to her.

Except to say that he'd missed her so much that it had ached. A physical pain in his body that wasn't relieved by exercise or work, sleep or alcohol.

Her mouth found his, again and again. All his words left him. There was only Simone and skin and warmth and this room.

Coronation? What coronation?

Constitutional crisis? What constitutional crisis?

Her fingers were at his waistband again, expertly undoing his belt and his trousers.

Manoeuvring his trousers at this stage of his arousal needed a gentle touch, and when her fingers touched him he reached down and held her hand.

He'd been waiting so long he knew that if she touched him there he might just come apart.

'Is everything all right?' she asked.

'Everything's wonderful.'

He wriggled his way out of his underpants and then pulled her back to him. For a brief second he thought about slowing down and taking their time. This was the first time they'd made love. They should be savouring, lingering… But maybe she felt, like him, that they were already making up for lost time. This hadn't been five minutes in the making. It had been three months. Their lives had been on pause since their last kiss.

Things were building inside him…sweet and, oh, so strong.

He felt himself being nudged in the direction of her bedroom, but her mouth didn't leave his. They were having a new type of conversation with their lips. No less meaningful than any they had had with actual words in the past.

I want you. I need you. Don't stop. Yes. There. Please.

She kicked the bedroom door closed with a satisfying bang and they tumbled onto her bed. His lips sought out her breasts and took a hard nipple into his mouth. She moaned, and he could feel her sighing. She was barely holding herself together, just like him. His tongue and her nipples were a magical, combustible combination.

Her hips bucked beneath him and the sheets bunched in her hands. She was as ready as he was, and it made him feel more powerful than any title they might bestow upon him.

'Ed… Ed, for the sake of your kingdom, please tell me you've got protection.'

Her question momentarily snapped him back to reality. The royal family already had one unexpected child on the way—they did not need another.

'Yes,' he panted, and dragged his body away from hers. 'Wallet.'

He hadn't come to see her with the intention of seducing her, but a part of him clearly hadn't ruled it out entirely.

Simone sat up on her bed with her blonde hair tousled around her flushed face. She grinned at him, temporarily halting his mission. He knelt back on the bed and kissed her again. He couldn't get enough.

A low murmur escaped her lips and she pushed him away. 'Have you forgotten what you were doing?' she asked.

He climbed off the bed and opened the door, hearing Simone whistle as she watched him from behind. With relief he saw that the living room was still unoccupied. He grabbed his trousers and went back to the bedroom. He found his wallet and the protection it contained. Ripped the packet as he rushed back to her.

She took his hand and the packet. 'Let me...' she murmured.

He had to bite back a moan as he watched her delicate fingers sheath him, trying his hardest not to come apart in her hands.

'I want you...' She nuzzled his neck.

'I want you.'

All of you. Always.

But he didn't say that to her. He barely acknowledged the thought to himself. It was too big, too much, considering the task that now lay before him. Not falling apart before she did. Not making a right royal mess of their first time together.

He must have paused too long with the thought, because Simone tugged at him, took his face in her hands and looked him straight in the eye. Then she adjusted herself, guiding him into her.

Her eyes half-closed, mouth half-open, she surrendered herself completely to him. There was a thin sheen of perspiration on her forehead. Her lips were swollen as he brought her to the brink.

Once they were as one, he didn't want it to end. This was his true destiny.

The rest of the world stopped and it was just them. Nothing else mattered. Not duty. Time. Nothing but Simone. They wound each other so perfectly tight and reached a perfect peak before they both found release. They held each other as they tumbled, fell, and came completely undone.

CHAPTER ELEVEN

IT WAS AS if she'd just woken up from an erotic dream. Disorientated, breathless, hot. And very confused.

Because this wasn't a dream.

It was a very real encounter.

Ed was next to her, also catching his breath, warm and trembling.

She rested her head against his chest and he pulled her against him, each anchoring the other as the waves of pleasure continued to wash through them.

She brought her breath in time with his and enjoyed the feeling of his firm chest against her cheek.

You've just made love with the King, a little voice whispered in her head.

But she dismissed it easily. He might be the King, but he was still just Ed too.

You've just made love with Ed.

She was incapable of moving even an inch because of the happy chemicals still thumping through her body.

And the shock.

And Ed's arm, flung across her, trapping her where she'd fallen.

His breathing was heavy, his face sweaty. His head tipped back and he looked up at the ceiling as he groaned.

'Oh, Sim. I can't believe we've only just realised we could do that.'

She was in real trouble.

Over the years Simone had often sought solace in the thought that maybe Ed wasn't very good in bed. That maybe they weren't physically compatible. It hadn't been a silly thought. They were relaxed in one another's company, and ease in public didn't always translate into heat in the bedroom. It might just as easily lead to something very bland. Maybe Ed, under his suits and underwear, was really not that much...

How wrong she had been.

Not only was Ed really all that and more under his clothes, he had also been at constant pains to please her. She shouldn't be surprised. He was her kind and caring friend. But, strangely, she had expected him to be more selfish in bed than he was. And Ed had most definitely been generous. Over and over again.

Her heart was in more danger than ever.

Ed isn't going to marry, and you aren't going to marry a prince.

No one, least of all Ed, was talking about marriage. This was just a one-off. Completing what they had started in Paris. That was all. A fling.

Can you really have an emotion-free fling with Ed?

She was about to find out.

'You know what I said in Paris?' he murmured.

He'd said so many things in Paris, but she knew what he meant.

'Do you think we've just ruined our friendship?'

'No, I don't feel differently about you,' she said honestly.

So many things had changed between them in the past few months. She cared for him as much as ever, but her emotions were closer to the surface, instead of being safely locked away.

He made a face. 'Really? Then I needed to try harder. Can I have another go?'

She laughed, but he didn't. His face was still calm and serious.

'Do you…feel differently about me?' she asked.

'I've felt differently since Paris,' he replied.

Her stomach swooped. 'What do you mean?'

She was afraid she wouldn't hear his answer over the roar of blood rushing past her ears.

'We haven't seen much of one another over the years.' His gaze fell on her bare shoulder and on his thumb, stroking it. 'I forgot…or rather…maybe I'm seeing you for the first time.'

She couldn't speak. They were words she'd dreamt of him saying. Ever since she was sixteen and had stood up in front of a room of people to sing to him. To tell him she loved him without saying the words.

'And for you? Was this too much of a surprise?' he asked.

'Definitely a surprise.' *You have no idea.* 'But a good one,' she added quickly.

A surprise. In the same way that winning the lottery was a surprise. Something you dreamt of, but never expected to actually happen.

'I'm glad to hear it.'

Ed tipped his head towards her and pressed his lips to hers. Pleasure slid down her spine. Not just because it felt wonderful, but because of the ease with which he did it. As if it was the most natural thing in the world to be kissing one another. Lying here, with him, placing languid kisses on one another was like a dream. Literally. She'd had this dream several, sweaty, discombobulating times in the past few months.

'What's it like?' she asked.

'Being with you? Wonderful.'

She swatted him gently.

'I meant being the King.'

'Oh, that. Not nearly as fun as what we just did.'

She smiled against his chest. For a moment he was hers. Just hers.

'I'm serious, though. Now I'm here you can tell me. How's it been? Really?'

'Busy. Stressful. Lonely.'

She tightened her embrace around him. For this moment at least he wouldn't be lonely. At this moment everything was as it should be.

They lay like that for a while. Talking, laughing, touching one another. The distant sound of a trumpet playing somewhere in the palace reminded her.

'Don't you have a kingdom to run?' she asked.

'Do I? I'd forgotten.'

His joking was sweet, and for a few precious moments she felt like the most important thing in the world to him.

But they both knew it couldn't last.

'You can't forget,' she said.

'I know, but it would be nice, wouldn't it?'

She propped herself up and looked at him. 'Yes, but it's just a fantasy. We both know it's fun to think about from time to time, but you have your life and I have mine.'

Ed's eyes darkened as he held her gaze. 'How long are you here for?'

'A week. I leave two days after your coronation.'

He grimaced, as if she'd reminded him of an execution and not of what should be one of the proudest days of his life.

'I'd like to see you again,' he said.

Again. The word shocked her back to the present and the reality they had forgotten for the past few hours.

Simone spun her legs off the edge of the bed and grabbed the nearest piece of clothing—her pyjama top, discarded hours earlier—and pulled it to her. The happy hormones had worn off and she'd hit the cold wall of reality with a thud.

She tugged the top over her head.

It was all very well to let herself get swept away with Ed and how wonderful it felt being with him, but they had to return to the real world. The one where he was the King of a country in crisis and she had built her own life and her own business in Paris.

Ed sat up. His gorgeous bare torso taunted her from her messed-up bed. Begging her to slide her hands over it and feel its hard magnificence.

'What's the matter?' he asked.

'It can't happen again.'

She searched her bedroom floor for some other clothes. Something to cover her bottom half. Suddenly she was feeling too naked. It was all very well to walk around the apartment naked when they were in the throes of passion, but now that they had to redraw the lines of their relationship she was feeling too exposed.

Protecting her heart was now her first priority.

'As wonderful as this was, you know we can't do this again.'

For a heartbeat, part of her hoped he'd argue with her, but he didn't.

'Can we see each other as friends?'

'I don't know.'

It was an honest answer. She didn't know how she could possibly sit across a table from him or on a sofa and talk to him while not thinking about what they had just done. She could still feel his mouth on her most sensitive parts. Her mind was still full of the memory of him moving so strongly and beautifully inside her. Her muscles were still trembling.

The answer on her lips was, *No. We can't. Because if we do I won't be able to push these feel-*

ings back down again. You are so close to breaking me completely.

It hurt to even think it.

'Simone, I'm not just going to walk out of here without a plan to see you again. I don't want us to do the awkward silence thing again. The last few months…not knowing if I should call you or not… have been awful.'

She put her face in her hands so she wouldn't have to look him in the eyes and see the pain written across them.

Could they be friends?

Can you imagine not being friends with Ed?

And that was it, wasn't it? She couldn't really conceive of a future that he wasn't part of in some way.

'Tonight?' she said.

'Tonight I have an official government dinner.'

And there it was. It wasn't his fault, but his duty would always come first. As it should. She hung her head.

'Tomorrow, though. I can cancel my plans tomorrow night.'

She shook her head. 'Ed, this is hard enough as it is. We both know this is impossible. *We're* impossible. I don't think we should make things any harder than they already are.'

'I have a few hours tomorrow afternoon, I think.'

She laughed. 'Ed, face it. Your life isn't yours any more. I don't want to make things harder for you.'

Or for me.

'You don't even want to spend time with me?' he asked.

It was so hard to explain that she did want to be with him, but she also didn't. It sounded foolish, but there it was. She was torn in two.

'Of course I want to spend time with you. But things just got complicated, didn't they?'

She looked down. She was wearing only her pyjama top and her panties from yesterday. She couldn't even dress herself, she was in such a state.

'You said nothing had changed,' he said.

'What?'

'A moment ago, you said your feelings hadn't changed.'

A moment ago her body had still been flooded with endorphins. Now reality had broken through.

'I spoke too quickly. Besides, it doesn't matter how I feel. The world has changed. The situation is different. You're the King.'

'I'm still me.'

His voice was small. Not at all regal. And it broke her heart.

How could she reconcile this monarch, the figurehead of his country, with the boy she'd always known?

It didn't matter if she could or not. She simply had to. They both had to.

And they both had to realise that this thing between them—whatever it was—belonged to their old lives and not their new futures.

'I know.' She knelt on the bed and took his face in her hands, cradling it. God, he was beautiful. 'I know. But we can't change what's happened. You have your duty and I won't let you jeopardise that for me. Besides, we both know I don't belong here.'

'Sim…'

His words petered out and they both knew there was nothing left to say. She left the bedroom and him to go and get dressed.

A few minutes later he emerged from the room, fully dressed and ready for a day of official duties. Looking as if nothing had just happened.

He kissed her quickly on the cheek. 'We'll figure something out. I promise.'

She nodded, but didn't believe him.

It was late morning—not even lunchtime—but to her body clock it felt like the middle of the night. She felt as if she'd lived a thousand hours, yet in real life it was no more than four.

That was the effect Ed had on her.

She wandered around the apartment, looking at her mother's things. Ceramic figurines that had belonged to Simone's grandmother, a framed photograph of Simone's mother and father on their wedding day.

She picked it up and held it closer to study it. It was slightly yellow, older than Simone herself. They looked happy. They had loved each other. And if cancer hadn't taken her father too soon they would still be together. Simone was sure of it. After all, Alea had never remarried. Until the last two or three years Alea hadn't even considered dating anyone.

Simone put down the frame and picked up the next photograph. It was of her and Ed, posing with Suzette. They couldn't have been older than ten. She didn't remember the photo being taken, but she remembered the jeans and bright stripy sweater she'd been wearing.

This was why she didn't come back here. It felt and smelt like her childhood, and those memories were overwhelming. Because they were all memories of Ed.

Happy memories, to be sure. Her happiest. Of waiting for Ed to come by. Of playing in the garden with him. Of sitting on her couch—this very couch—watching television with him. Of playing video games. Of playing with Suzette.

Suzette the cocker spaniel. She'd been a deep golden brown that had faded as she'd got older. She had been one of the first beings to meet her here when Simone had first arrived, still reeling and confused after her father's death. Not quite understanding the enormity and significance of their move, she'd been excited to be moving to an actual palace. She'd loved her new bedroom at first sight, and then she had seen the garden from her window.

She'd rushed down and found Suzette.

A puppy! She'd always wanted a dog.

The palace really had seemed like a fairy tale. And then the boy had come along. She hadn't known he was the Prince at first. In fact, she hadn't realised that for a while. He'd just been Ed. A boy about her own age who had told her where the balls were, to throw to Suzette, and shown her all the secrets of the garden.

Simone fell asleep on the sofa. But even her dreams were about her childhood.

Another memory. She was fourteen. The last day of the school year. She'd come home from school, sad to be saying goodbye to her friends for the summer, but glad that Ed was returning from boarding school. And there he'd been, in the palace kitchen, talking to her mother. And eating. Because that was what fifteen-year-old boys did.

And no wonder. When he'd stood up she'd seen that he was nearly a foot taller than he'd been in the winter. Clean, soft face. A jawline that was starting to firm up. Shoulders that were broader and straighter than when she'd seen him last. But still the same deep green eyes that reminded her of the evergreen trees that grew in the garden. When he'd smiled her stomach had flipped. A new and strange sensation.

I love him, her fourteen-year-old self had thought.

She might have been young, but she'd *known*. She'd known in her heart that she loved this boy like her own soul, and would never stop loving him.

And then suddenly they were in the summer house, and everyone was laughing and pointing at her. Mocking her singing. She tried to get out of the room, but people kept blocking her way. And laughing. Laughing. Laughing...

CHAPTER TWELVE

ED HAD HIS dinner with the French Ambassador moved to lunch, and then cancelled some other appointments, saying he needed to preserve his energy for coronation day. It wasn't a lie, exactly. He was doing something for his own mental health by seeing Simone that night.

She didn't want them to sleep together again, and he not only respected that decision but reluctantly agreed that she was right. She was stronger than him. She was saving him from himself. Making sure that this thing between them—he didn't know what to call it—didn't get any more difficult than it already was.

He had to put his job first.

Duty first.

Wasn't that what being the King was really all about?

His father had spoken to him throughout his life about sacrifice—sacrifice for his country, his people, the greater good—and Ed had never understood. Being King would be an honour and even a pleasure, he'd thought. He wouldn't be giving up anything. Anonymity? He'd never had that anyway.

Now he understood. Now, not only did he understand in his head, but he felt it in his chest—the true meaning of sacrifice.

Simone would leave Florena after the coronation. Things would return to how they had been and it would get easier. It always did. Any time he said goodbye to a woman it hurt for a while and then it got better.

Simone's been the last thing you think of each night and the first each morning since you got back from Paris.

He conceded that might be true, but that was just due to their unfinished business in Paris. The rude interruption of his father's abdication. Now that they had scratched that itch—so to speak—things would return to the way they had been. Simone had made it clear there was no other choice.

And as usual she was right.

This brought him to Sara. His stylist, hairdresser and sometime make-up artist. Because, yes, he occasionally wore make up. For television appearances, mostly. Or official photographs. A light dusting of power to stop the glare of stage lights. Or some concealer to hide the effects of a big night.

He was a figurehead. If he didn't look healthy people talked. If he looked hungover they talked even more.

But now Sara paused when he made his request. 'Are you sure?'

He nodded and she set to work. In fact he was shocked with the enthusiasm with which she tackled her assignment. A few times she even laughed. She was enjoying herself way too much. And when he asked for recommendations as to where he could take an old friend for a night out she was equally obliging.

When she'd completed her handiwork, she even helped him choose an outfit and pad out his shoulders to complete the look.

When he stood in front of the mirror she cackled, patted him on the shoulder and wished him luck. 'I'll be keeping an eye on social media.'

'What?'

'Kidding. I'll resign if someone identifies you. I'd consider it a professional failure.'

Ed turned from side to side in front of the mirror. He was quite proud of his new nose. It was large. Any larger and it would be too distinctive. But it was balanced out by the wrinkles she'd given him. And the wart. He was less keen on the wart, but Sara had insisted.

She'd definitely got too much pleasure from making him look as if he was forty years older than he was, but he had been prepared to let her. She was doing him a favour. He wanted to show Simone that even after yesterday morning they were friends, first and foremost. No funny business. He wasn't taking her out to seduce her, but so they could have a friendly night together.

Simone would not be attracted to him looking as he did now. Like a seventy-year-old man with a gigantic nose and a wart on his chin. When he arrived at her door looking like this she would know that he was serious about their friendship. That he could accept that friends were all they would ever be.

Either that or she'd laugh.

It was very strange, walking through the palace made up as he was. No one bowed, but they did give him puzzled looks. Still, no one stopped him to ask who he was and what he was doing. Something he ought to bring up with his head of security.

Simone opened the door to the apartment and didn't speak for a long time. He didn't want to be recognised, but this was Simone! If she didn't recognise him he'd know that he was safe to go out in public.

But he'd also be strangely disappointed.

A few heartbeats passed before a smile crept over her face. 'Your Majesty.'

'What gave me away?'

'What do you mean? You look exactly like you did yesterday morning. Only now you look like you had a good night's sleep.'

'Ha-ha.'

'What on earth are you doing?'

'I've come to ask if you would like to go out for a drink with me.'

She laughed. 'With you looking like that?'

'It's my disguise. The glasses might have worked in Paris, but here I need something a bit more.'

'That's definitely *more*. Who did you get to do it? Jim Henson?'

'Again, you're hilarious. My stylist—Sara. She was surprisingly happy to do it for me.'

Alea poked her head around the door, did a double-take, then laughed.

He stepped into the room and did a spin. 'What do you think?'

Alea was kinder than her daughter. 'It's only your voice that gives you away. If you don't speak, no one will know who you are.'

'Thank you.' He turned back to Simone. 'So, will you come with me?'

Simone turned to her mother, said they'd been planning on spending the evening together, but Alea waved her out through the door

'Go—have fun. You've been hanging out here all day. Go and have a good night.'

'I'm in my pyjamas,' Simone said.

Ed recognised the lovely curve-skimming silk set from Paris. He swallowed.

'So go and change!' Ed and Alea said in unison.

Simone pulled on some fitted black trousers and a soft, loose white sweater. She examined herself in the mirror. It was just a casual night out. There was no need to go overboard. But then she remembered the last time she'd gone to one of Florena's bars and she pulled down a box from the top of her wardrobe.

It was her old dressing up box. Full of odd but fun items that she and Alea had collected over the years. She took out the short dark wig she had worn to a fancy dress party when she had gone as Lois Lane. She tucked her long blonde hair up inside it and put on some lipstick.

She hardly recognised herself.

'Hey, why do *you* need a disguise?' Ed said when she emerged from her room.

'It's hardly the same as yours,' she said, as they made their way to the back door of the palace.

'But still… Why?'

She should be honest with him. This was still Ed.

'Once, a few years ago, I went out in the old town with Mum. I was photographed. And…well, they linked photos of me with that video and piled on the abuse. I know it isn't anything like what you have to endure, but I'd rather wear the wig.'

And if Ed was recognised her name might be published next to his.

She didn't tell him that, though, because it would sound as if she was ashamed to be with him. Which she wasn't.

She was protecting them both.

Ed frowned, but picked up her gloved hand and squeezed it. Simone looked around the quiet street. There was no one around. For a few minutes they walked along the road like any normal couple.

The moment ended when they reached the old town. Despite the cold and the late hour, the cobble-stoned streets were still full of people and Simone dropped Ed's hand. The Christmas decorations had been taken down and replaced with bunting for the coronation. Flags of red and white—Florena's national colours—hung in strings across the streets. Fairy lights adorned half the houses. The other half were strung with garlands of evergreen branches.

The shopfronts were decorated too. A string of bejewelled paper crowns hung in the window of an old sweet shop. The next shop was a cake shop, with a large cake shaped like a crown in its window and a display of cupcakes making up the Florenan flag. It seemed every shopfront on the cobblestoned street was preparing for the coronation.

'It's amazing,' Simone said.

Ed nodded.

'This is all for you,' she whispered. 'Can you get your head around it? I'm not sure that I can.'

'No, I can't. It's like there are two of me,' he said. 'The King and Ed.'

She nodded and turned. 'Duty first.'

He reached for her hand again and drew her to him. Even that small, innocent gesture felt risky, standing where they were.

'Don't forget, Simone. I'm still Ed. I'm still your Ed.'

She nodded, though she didn't agree.

Ed showed her into a nearby old-style pub. It was small, with low ceilings and a roaring fire. Simone ordered their drinks, both judging it best if Ed did as little speaking to others as possible, and they found a quiet table near the back.

Candles lit the table, but even in the low light she could still make out the sparkle in Ed's eyes.

Even with the make-up he was still handsome.

You will still adore him when he's old. There will never be a time when you are not attracted to him.

She shook her head.

'What are you thinking?' he asked.

She sighed. 'I'm thinking how unfair it is that you will probably still be handsome when you're seventy.'

Ed smiled, but then looked down. 'Do I look like my father? I'm worried I look like him.'

'Honestly, no. You don't. You look like your mother.'

He grinned. 'I'm sure she'd love to hear you say that right now.'

'Not now, silly, but in general. You have her eyes and her hair.'

'I feel I'm destined to be like him.' Ed's words were soft.

'You aren't like him.'

'Edouard the Fourth. Philanderer. Cheater. Playboy.'

'You aren't any of those things.'

Simone wanted to reach over the table and pick up his hand, and for a moment it felt as though she could, but she kept her hands tightly in her lap.

'You are your own person. A good person. And you will show everyone that. You will do your duty. You won't make your father's mistakes.'

You will not get involved with the palace crooner.

Simone continued. 'And your plan is the best one. Stay single. Stay loyal to your country. You will be like Elizabeth the First of England!'

Ed looked sombre. 'I really didn't ask you out tonight to talk about that. I simply wanted to have a night out with my best friend. Truly.'

They ordered another drink each and he told her about his parents and feeling trapped between them and their lawyers. He asked about the bookshop and about Paris. She told him about the TV shows she'd been bingeing, the books she'd come across. Everyday mundane things. For a moment she forgot where she was and why she was there. They drank, they laughed, and they pretended for a few precious hours to be just Simone and Ed.

But soon they made their way back through the streets and to the private gate of the palace. Entering without being noticed, they walked along an ancient colonnade that bounded one side of a small quadrangle at the side of the palace.

'Thank you for this evening,' he said.

'You don't have to thank me.'

'I do. Thank you for giving me a few hours of normality. For letting me pretend.'

'Oh Ed...'

A wave of emotion rushed through her. She wanted to make everything all right for him. She wanted to spend many evenings with him as they just had.

Before she could say anything he had slipped his arm around her waist and pulled her towards him. Their lips, cold at first from the walk, quickly warmed one another on the outside and from within. Her knees wobbled and he pushed her gently against the nearest wall for support.

It was exquisite.

It was tender.

It was too much.

'We shouldn't be doing this. Not here!'

His lips tugged on her lower lip and he let out a tortured groan. 'I know…but it feels so good.'

She felt so good.

Complete.

Home.

She dipped her head. *No.* Home was in Paris.

'Stay,' he said.

The word hung in the air. She was waiting for him to take it back. He was waiting for her answer.

'Not for ever,' he said.

She exhaled.

'Just a little longer…'

'I have to get back to the bookshop. To Paris. I can't come back here. You know that. Nothing's changed. If anything, it would be harder for me to stay here.'

'Why not just try it for a while? A month or two? That's all. Your mother would love it.'

The mention of her mother and the look in his pleading eyes made her chest ache.

'You know I don't feel at home here.'

'But this *is* your home.'

She sighed. She hated having to talk about that video. The mockery and the trolling.

'Ed, please, you're not being fair. Not to me. Or to yourself.'

He couldn't promise her for ever and she respected that—because she couldn't promise it either.

'Is it really about the video?'

'Yes, partly.'

'You shouldn't be worried about that.'

She cringed and stepped away from him. 'Stop joking. It isn't funny.'

'I'm not joking. You sounded fine. It's a difficult song and you weren't awful…'

'Wow, thanks.'

'Sim, you looked lovely. Beautiful. It was really sweet.'

A horrible uncomfortable thought crept over her. 'When was the last time you watched it?'

He bowed his head. 'Recently…'

She narrowed her eyes.

'Okay, maybe yesterday.'

'Yesterday! Why? It was the most embarrassing moment of my life and you're still watching it?'

She set off along the colonnade.

'Simone, I love watching it. I'm sorry, but I do. I love looking at any photo or video of you. I'm quite addicted.'

She stopped and looked across the courtyard at the towers of the palace. He liked her singing. It had taken thirteen years, but she'd finally charmed him. She let out a rueful laugh.

'Have *you* seen it lately?' he asked.

She shook her head.

'You should watch it. I think you might find that it isn't as embarrassing as you remember.'

But whether it was good or bad wasn't the point. The fact that it had made its way to the smartphone screens of everyone in Florena was mortifying. The fact that the photo of her clutching the microphone, mouth wide open and eyes half closed, had launched a thousand memes was enough to make anyone want to emigrate.

And then the online abuse… It had come right off social media and into her own inbox. Trolls, going out of their way to tell her how ugly she was. How stupid she was. How pathetic she was for throwing herself at the Prince. How she should probably end her own life.

'So it was embarrassing?' said Ed. 'We've all done drunk karaoke. We've all had embarrassing photos of us published. Join the club. Remember those photos of me with the Spanish models?'

She nodded. She remembered those photos all too well. 'It looked like you were enjoying yourself.'

'I'd had too much to drink, and I *was* enjoying myself, but the photos were out of context. It made it look like I was a second away from ripping their bikinis off with my teeth.'

She raised an eyebrow 'And were you?'

'No. Someone just took the photo at the wrong moment.'

She didn't want to think about Ed and the trio of Spanish models he'd been partying with. She also didn't want to think about the video. And what had followed.

She pulled her coat tight against the cold. 'They hate me here.'

'No, they don't.'

'They mocked me. Laughed at me. Some of them told me '

Some of them had told her to die. She couldn't even say it aloud.

The messages had continued for weeks. At first she'd changed her email address, and then her phone number. But the trolls had still found her. She'd eventually given up all social media. For a sixteen-year-old away from home that had been hard.

It had been weeks before she'd been able to sleep properly again. And all she'd done was to sing a song at a party. If people knew she had slept with the King… Then what? What sort of attacks would await her?

Even if she wanted to stay and put herself through that kind of humiliation again, she wasn't sure she physically could.

'I'm constantly worried that someone will make

fun of me, but I've had to learn to rise above it or I'd be paralysed,' Ed said.

'It's different for you. You're the King.'

He blinked. A long, confused blink.

'I'm nobody,' she clarified.

'You're not nobody.'

'But I'm not your Queen. Or even your girlfriend.'

She held her breath while she waited for him to answer. Half hoping and half dreading that he'd contradict her.

You could be my girlfriend. You could be my Queen.

But he didn't.

'I could protect you,' he said.

She sighed deeply. 'You couldn't the last time I hit the front page. No one could. I was sent away. Banished!'

Ed frowned. 'I was a kid then. I didn't know what had gone on. This time I'll protect you.'

'I was sent away. I was such an embarrassment to the palace that I was *sent away*.'

She was one more word away from breaking down.

'Is that what you think?' he asked.

'It's what I *know*. And you even think your father paid my school fees. That's how much they wanted to get rid of me.'

He groaned. 'That's not why you were sent away.'

'Then why?'

He looked at her for a long while before saying, 'I can't tell you why.'

She tugged on her gloves and tightened her scarf, which had been dislodged by their kiss. 'Because that *is* why. I was sent away in disgrace. Even though your father isn't around now, having me here would just give Laurent more ammunition. I have to leave for your sake.'

Ed laughed loudly. 'Bad karaoke singing is not scandalous enough to destroy the country. Even yours.'

Rage built inside her and it took every ounce of control not to scream at him. *Hysterical woman screams at King!* She could write the headline herself.

'The country turned on me—'

'It wasn't the entire country.'

'I wasn't welcome and…'

Her throat closed over. The things they'd said to her… She didn't want to stay and be abused again. Even for Ed.

They reached the door that led up to her apartment.

Ed stepped towards her with his hands out. Perfectly earnest. 'Simone, I'll protect you. It wouldn't be like last time.'

'It doesn't matter. My life's in Paris.'

It was lovely that he wanted to try, but they both knew that her fear of the spotlight was only one of their problems.

'I just wish you'd feel comfortable spending more time here. I don't want to upset you, but I want to keep talking about this. I understand there are many reasons why you wouldn't want to come back, but I don't want you to think that banishment is one of them.'

He leant down and kissed her cheek. His lips lingered and they breathed in each other's scent, as if to carry the memory away with them. Every time she had to say goodbye to him her heart broke a little more.

She turned and began to climb the stairs before she could change her mind.

Back in her room, she tugged off the wig and rubbed her itchy scalp.

He didn't understand what it was like for her. He was the King. He had people to check his social media. He had an army sworn to defend his honour. She'd been kicked out of the country the first time she'd done something wrong.

Even if she wasn't about to be deported again, would she be able to withstand the scrutiny and criticism that was sure to come her way if anyone got wind of the fact that she had slept with the King?

Did she even want to? Was it worth it?

You have to have a strong sense of yourself.

She did have a strong sense of herself. Much more so than when she was sixteen. She was Simone Auclair. She ran a second-hand bookshop in Paris. She loved books and reading and her mother. She loved her friends, Julia and André. She *knew* who she was.

And if she didn't have Paris and her bookshop then who was she? Her mother's daughter? Ed's friend?

She didn't want to be defined by being Ed's girlfriend. Once upon a time that might have been a dream come true, but if that was how she defined herself and then it was taken away from her…? Then who would she be?

Because if she didn't even know who she was, she certainly wouldn't be able to withstand the trolls.

CHAPTER THIRTEEN

AFTER A MEETING to decide on the final details of the coronation, and when he'd finished signing the box of papers for the day, his staff left him alone. Ed took out his phone and brought up the video of Simone singing. He watched it more regularly than he'd like to admit to anyone.

Remembering her words from last night, he didn't click on the link. To her, it was a betrayal for him to watch the video.

Simone in his arms was everything he'd never known he wanted—no, needed. All the dreams he'd been too afraid to picture.

She's your best friend, and for a precious morning was your lover.

His overwhelming thought after making love with Simone had been that she was the only person in the world he should be doing it with. That everything else in his life up to that point had been not quite right.

He'd put Simone into a mental box. Childhood best friend. And for years he'd kept her there, convinced that that was the only place for her.

Until Paris.

Until he'd finally seen her as the woman she was.

And now there was no going back.

Not that he wanted to. This Simone—this woman who'd lain with him the other morning—was magnificent. Soft and firm in all the right places. Warm and loving and everything he'd never even let himself imagine a lover could be.

Now when he clicked on the video he did feel he was betraying her by doing so. She had been genuinely traumatised by the fallout. She had been young. She'd had to deal with it alone. Worst of all, she genuinely believed that she had been banished from Florena because of it.

What a mess. If only she understood that she'd been sent away to boarding school because of the affair between his father and her mother and that it had nothing to do with the video. If only he could make her understand that… Clearly Alea had not divulged that secret.

For the first time Ed did more than glance at the comments below the video. There were thousands of them. Some complimentary, but most were vile. He'd dealt with online bullies in his time, but the vitriol reserved for women was on a different level entirely. And aimed at a sixteen-year-old girl?

Thank goodness he'd never have a daughter of his own. He didn't have the slightest idea how he'd prepare her for what she was likely to face from the trolls of the world as Princess of Florena.

Still, he didn't put his phone away and considered rewatching the video. Because Simone was gorgeous, and lovely, and her voice played on his heart strings like a maestro. Her singing was heartfelt…as if she was singing to someone.

Maybe he was a little obsessed.

But he was also curious.

Why had she been she singing? Why *that* song? Karaoke had been her idea. But something didn't feel right. It didn't feel like Simone. She wasn't a show-off. She wasn't shy, but usually she took a little persuading to put herself forward in a group where she didn't know many people. She must have had a well thought-out reason for singing.

You've been asking the wrong question. The right question is who was she singing to?

She hadn't known anyone at the party apart from her mother and the senior staff who had always been invited to those events. The rest of the guests had been either his friends or his parents' friends. Simone hadn't known most of those people. Ed hadn't even known many of those people.

Which meant…

His veins turned to ice and he froze.

He was such an idiot.

A special kind of stupid.

Seventeen-year-old boy stupid.

He couldn't believe he'd assumed that Simone's feelings for him had been running parallel with his. That they had only begun seriously in Paris, when his own feelings had.

But what if she had loved him…for ever?

When she'd declined his invitation to come back to Florena with him after the abdication he'd assumed it was because she didn't have feelings for him. Or that any feelings she did have were not strong enough.

But what if it wasn't that at all?

All this time he'd been thinking he'd just been reckless with his own feelings. Risking his own heart. That was one thing, but he realised shamefully that he'd been careless with hers too. He had assumed that he was the only one in danger of being hurt.

You don't know how she feels about you. You don't know anything for sure.

But it might explain why she'd been so upset about the fallout from the video. It might explain why she'd been so reluctant to come back to Florena. He knew she'd been upset by the trolls and didn't want to risk further humiliation. And she thought she'd been banished once before. Those were all real fears and concerns.

But all this time he'd been assuming that her feelings for him were not strong enough to help her overcome those fears.

But what if he was wrong? What if it was the complete opposite and she didn't want to return precisely because she had feelings for him?

He took off his tie and jacket and threw on his casual sweater.

Even if he was a monarch, he could still be diabolically stupid.

Simone spent the afternoon in the kitchen, helping chop vegetables, cut pastry and wash dishes. Anything the kitchen staff would let her do to keep her mind off what had been happening between her and Ed.

Her mother had hired additional hands to handle the influx of guests over the coronation weekend and to cover for her. As the manager of the kitchen Alea was invited to the coronation and the ball, but she still had to co-ordinate the catering.

The kitchen work might not have kept her mind completely away from Ed. Or his hands. Or the things he could do with his tongue. But at least it had kept her from doing anything stupid. Like calling up André and asking him to run the bookshop on a permanent basis while she lived the rest of her life locked away in the palace as the King's secret mistress.

Of course she'd never do that.

Like everything else it was a silly fantasy. But now she was elbow-deep in grimy water, reminding herself that being with Ed in the long term and keeping her sanity were two diametrically opposed outcomes.

The large kitchen, which had been filled with laughter and chatter, suddenly fell silent behind her. She looked around to see what the problem was. Ed was walking towards her through a wave of bows and mutterings of 'Your Majesty'.

As he approached her he grinned, almost shyly. But that couldn't be right.

He was never shy around anyone—least of all her. When he reached her, she bowed too.

'Simone, would you like to have a walk with me?'

'I'm…' She was about to tell him she was busy and refuse his invitation, but then she saw all the eyes trained on her. 'Certainly, Your Majesty.'

He raised an eyebrow.

Simone dried her hands and followed him out of the kitchen. When they were out of earshot he said, 'What was all that about? The bowing…the "Your Majesty"?'

'In case you've forgotten, you're the King. If I don't bow people will want to know why. If I don't call you "Your Majesty" people will pretty much assume we're sleeping together.'

'They know we're friends.'

'The old staff do. But not the temporary staff here for the coronation.'

'They've all signed NDAs.'

'That's not the point, Ed.'

He stopped walking and grabbed her arm, so she stopped too.

'What *is* the point? Do you not want to see me?'

She sighed. 'We just need to be careful. And you know that more than anyone.'

He nodded. 'I don't know what I'd do without you,' he said.

She laughed wryly. 'You'll be just fine.'

Future tense. His life would go on perfectly smoothly and scandal-free once she'd left.

Hers, on the other hand…? She would be the one piecing her broken heart back together.

They reached the door to the garden and looked out. It had begun to snow. She looked down at her outfit. A long dress, tights and a long cardigan. He wasn't suitably attired either, with his dress shoes and only a thin sweater.

'It's too cold outside. Will you come to my room?'

This had now progressed from a casual walk and talk to a visit to his private rooms.

'Ed. I... I thought we'd talked about this. I'm not going to be the nearest warm body,' she whispered.

'What? You think I want to be with you just because you are close and warm?'

She glanced at the butler coming towards him and motioned for him to lower his voice.

'We're *definitely* going to my room for this conversation.'

He took her hand and pulled her in the direction of the royal apartments. She shook his hand away—but followed him anyway.

They walked quickly in silence to his room, greeting each person they passed with an overly friendly hello.

His apartment had a spacious sitting room, an office space, and an oversized bedroom. It was the same one he'd had for ever.

'Will you move into the King's apartments?' she asked.

He glared at her. 'Not the time, Simone. What did you mean, you don't want to be the nearest warm body?'

'Well… I didn't mean exactly that. But Paris…? The other morning…? And now you've brought me to your apartments.'

My heart may not be as important as a country, but I need it to live and breathe.

'I kissed you in Paris because I wanted to. I slept with you the other day because I've been dreaming about it since I left Paris. And because I wanted to—very much. Because after having you as my friend for so long…after so many years of taking you for granted as my friend… I finally see what an amazing and beautiful woman you are. I know I was slow on that account, but there you go.'

She could only stare. Amazing and beautiful woman?

'And, for the record, I don't just go around sleeping with women because they are close and warm. Do you actually believe what they print about me?'

She bit her lip. 'I don't…'

His look challenged her. She might as well get all her insecurities out into the open.

'But I know you've been with a lot of women, that's all.'

He let out a cynical guffaw.

'That's what you think of me? After everything you know about royal life, you still believe the headlines?'

'I don't need a number, Ed, but I see the photographs. I try my best not to see *all* the photographs, but I see them. And even if you only slept with a fraction of them, then…'

What? She'd run out of words. And she'd said too much.

He moved back to her. 'You try not to see the photographs? What do you mean by that?'

His voice was kind, and he raised a gentle eyebrow.

'Because…because I care about you, Ed.'

He encircled her in his arms and she pressed her face to his chest, so he wouldn't see the colour in her cheeks.

'Now we're getting somewhere. "Care…"?'

'Care is as much as you're getting now. We're friends. I like to know what you're up to.'

He pulled back to look at her with a broad smile. 'Again, for the record, it's not even a fraction of what the press would have you believe. And I do like it that you are close. And do I like that you are warm. But even if you weren't I'd still want to do this.'

He brushed his lips across hers.

She closed her eyes and breathed him in. There was no denying he was close…and very, very warm.

She let his speech run through her head a few more times, conscious that his hands were sliding up her back, sliding over the sensitive skin on her neck. Making her shiver.

'I've been dreaming about it since I left Paris… I finally see what a beautiful and amazing woman you are…'

She opened her eyes and sought out his lips.

CHAPTER FOURTEEN

THE KISS GREW deeper as they both fell into it. Fingers in each other's hair. Hands under one another's clothes. Tongues encircling one another's.

All the air left Simone's body and with it all her inhibitions.

She grabbed at the hem of Ed's sweater. Tugging. Pulling it out of the way. And he did the same with the buttons down the front of the dress she was wearing. He lifted her backside onto the nearest desk and she finally got his sweater over his head.

Ed pushed her lacy bra down, lifting and exposing one swollen, tender breast and taking it into his mouth. He kissed her painfully hard nipple and the room spun around her. He slid his hand up her thigh. Higher and higher.

Desperate need pooled inside her and came close to overflowing. She pushed him away. Very conscious of the fact they were in his apartment, not hers. And on his desk, no less.

'What if someone comes in?'

'They won't.'

'But…'

'Come.' He took her hand and led her to the other room. His bedroom. He shut the door behind him. 'I'm still just Ed. This is still my room.'

Simone swallowed hard. He was right. Ed was in front of her. Pulling her towards his bed and everything she'd always wanted. She just had to find the courage to take it.

He stepped back to her, shirt awry. She reached out and undid the last of his buttons, ran her hand over his chest and slipped the shirt over his magnificent shoulders. She threw it to the ground and reached for his belt buckle.

'Don't rush. I want to savour every second of this.'

The subtext was that this might be the last time. It might not have been what he meant, but it was what she heard.

And he was right. If this was to be the last time she would commit every second to memory. Every caress, every stroke, every sensuous lick.

Ed kissed her all over as he slid her dress away, coaxed her bra off and eased her panties down. Waves and waves of pleasure washed through her.

She slowly divested him of the rest of his clothes. Committing each inch of his body to memory and each inch to her lips. She consumed his addictive scent, surrendered her body to him and was worshipped in return.

He trembled as he said her name.

'Yes. Yes...' she replied.

Protected and on the brink, they finally came together.

She closed her eyes and let go. Desire gathering, tightening, hardening...finally breaking apart. All her being seemed to concentrate on this one moment of perfect, terrifying clarity. She'd love him no matter who he was. She'd love him until the end of time.

She broke and so did he.

They lay in one another's arms, spent and satiated. For the first time since the other morning Ed felt normal and content. Like himself. And that was all because of Simone.

'I have a question for you,' he said after a while.

He felt her body tense in his arms. She knew him well enough to know that his question was going to be serious.

'Why were you singing? At my party?'

'Oh, that… I don't remember.'

'I don't believe that for a second.' He said it gently, but felt her body stay frozen nonetheless.

'We went over this before. You've got to get back to work and I'd better get back to Mum.'

'What are you not telling me? It wasn't like you to put yourself out there in front of a whole lot of people you didn't know. Why did you?'

He stroked her hair and felt her shift under him.

'I had a crush on you,' she mumbled into his chest.

He'd guessed as much, but to hear her say it still stirred up many emotions. Surprise, delight, worry…

'You *had* a crush on me? Past tense?'

She groaned, as if it was something to be ashamed of.

'Because *my* crush is very much in the present

tense. Just so you know. And I'm not embarrassed in the slightest,' he said.

She giggled, and lifted herself up to look at him. Her blonde hair was tossed around her shoulders. Her lips still red and swollen from their kissing. She took his breath away. She was beautiful and she was Simone. *His* Simone.

'Yes, I had a teenage crush on you. Along with every other girl. Except it was mortifying because you were my best friend. You knew me and didn't share my feelings. Everyone knew how pathetic I was. That's why they sent me away.'

He couldn't believe that she believed everything she was saying.

He took her chin in his fingers. 'Simone, no. That's not why you were sent away at all. No one knows you had a crush on me!'

'They mocked me for singing to you.'

He rubbed his head. Was that really true? How could her recollections be so different from his?

'I think they were just laughing at the video. I don't think anyone thought you were singing to me.'

'Hashtag *palaceserenade*? That's pretty clear to me.'

'But…' It hadn't been clear to him. He sighed and bit his lip. He'd failed to notice a lot of things. 'Simone, I'm sorry I didn't notice.'

'You weren't meant to. I mean, you were only meant to realise if you shared my feelings. And I thought it worked, and you hadn't realised, and it all would have been fine except that then someone posted the video and made fun of it and everyone saw.'

The way she was talking in the past tense was starting to worry him. Was she over him? Had her feelings dissipated over the years, just as his were growing?

'Does any of it remain? Your teenage crush?'

She grinned. 'Ah, I don't know. My teenage crush was very…chaste.'

He laughed.

'This is something new.'

She trailed a finger down his chest and slid her hand under the covers. Just the thought of her fingers encircling him was enough to make his body react.

His fingers slid into her thick hair. He cradled her head and tilted her face towards him.

Something new.

But what?

It was powerful. And wonderful. But also dangerous.

This wasn't a chaste teenage crush or even an unchaste one. This was real life—both their lives—not to mention the future of his country.

He knew that. He knew that by continuing to be with Simone like this he could be putting all his carefully laid plans at risk.

Stay away from any hint of scandal. Be a monarch above all reproach. Beyond any criticism at all.

But this was Simone. She was next to him now and he needed her more than he needed air. No one needed to know. This would just be between them. She'd go back to Paris. He'd vowed to fulfil his royal duties alone. She didn't want to stay in Florena, and he accepted that, but that didn't mean they couldn't both make the most of this brief interlude in their lives.

Ed took a deep breath and knocked on the familiar apartment door. He heard movement inside and the door opened.

Alea smiled when she saw him. 'Eddie, sweetheart, come on in.'

He was instantly grateful that she had greeted him as usual, and hadn't curtsied or called him by his new title.

'It's lovely to see you,' she said.

'You too.'

'I'm afraid you've missed Simone. She's out having her dress fitted.'

'I confess I knew that. It's you I've come to see.'

Ed's throat was dry. Alea was one of the people in the world he felt most comfortable with, but what he'd come to ask was…delicate. He'd thought about coming weeks ago, before Simone had returned, and every day since then. But he wasn't sure what Simone had told her mother about the developments in their relationship. And he wasn't sure how she was going to react to his impertinent request.

'That sounds slightly ominous… Eddie, you know you're welcome here any time. Do you have time for a coffee?' she asked.

He nodded. They made small talk until the coffee was brewed, placed on the table with milk and sugar.

The coffee was sweet and robust, as always. Alea was a magnificent cook. But he was delaying. None of his etiquette lessons had ever taught him the art of raising one of his father's affairs with one of his old mistresses.

'I was wondering…that is… I don't think Simone knows about your affair with my father.'

There. No going back now.

Alea placed her cup down. 'I don't think she does either.'

'I was wondering if you had planned to tell her.'

'I hadn't really thought about it.' She crossed her arms.

'I wonder if you would like to think about it, now she's older.'

'Honestly, I'm not sure I planned to keep it a secret from her for ever, but it's in the past. You know that. Your father and I haven't been together for years. I don't think there's any need to dredge up the past. Particularly not now, with Celine and everything.'

'I know that. But I think maybe Simone deserves to know.'

'Eddie, I don't regret being with your father. You

know it ended amicably between us. No harm done. You're an adult now. Old enough to know that people need company. People need touch. Companionship.'

Ed ran his hand over his head. This wasn't what he'd come to hear from Simone's mother.

'Alea, please, *please* don't think for a moment I'm judging you. I do understand. That's not it.'

'Then why raise it now?'

'Ordinarily I wouldn't, but Simone and I have...'

This was dangerous ground too.

Alea narrowed her eyes.

'Simone and I are close.'

'You always have been.'

'Yes, but recently I've realised we have this secret between us.'

'You've always kept this from her—what's changed now?'

No. Simone clearly hadn't discussed their relationship with her mother. Alea was smart, and she had probably guessed, but she was wanting confirmation. This was harder than he'd thought it would be.

'It's important to me that there aren't any secrets between Simone and I.'

That explanation would have to do. He wasn't about to tell Alea that he was sleeping with her daughter—especially as Simone hadn't.

Besides, she might ask him about his intentions, and he wasn't sure that he could use the 'we're both consenting adults' speech back to her.

'It isn't your secret. It's mine and your father's.'

'I know. Which is why I'm coming to you and not Simone. The thing is, she believes she was sent away from the palace because of that video of her singing.'

'What video?' Alea asked.

'The one of her singing karaoke at my seventeenth birthday.'

'Where she sang *I Will Always Love You*?'

'Yes.'

'But that's absurd.'

'Yes, that's what I thought. But the clip went viral and she got a lot of horrible online abuse because of it.'

'But that wasn't why she was sent to school. The events were not connected.'

'I know that. But the timing was close and she never knew about the affair. It's what she believes, and I can see why she might. Rightly or wrongly, the abuse she received because of that video is one of the reasons she doesn't like coming back here.'

Alea paled. 'Really?'

'Yes—and it's why she plans on going back to Paris as soon as the coronation is over.'

Alea waved his suggestion away. 'She has a bookshop to manage. She always has to go back.'

'I want her to stay,' he said. 'Don't you?'

Alea held her face in her hands. 'Of course I do. And you're right. She should know the full story.'

Ed nodded, but then Alea shook her head and stood. She began to pace.

'But it isn't as simple as you suggest. We've all put it behind us. Your father, me, your mother… Even you. I know you and your mother accepted it as the way things were, but I don't know if Simone will.'

Ed hadn't been happy about the affair, but as his mother had accepted the relationship he hadn't felt it was his place to rock the boat.

'I'm not sure we should dig up the past. It's over,' Alea continued.

But not for Simone. And not for him.

'Please talk to her. If you won't do it for me, maybe you should do it for you.'

Alea frowned.

'I thought you should know,' Ed said, before downing the last of his coffee and taking his leave.

CHAPTER FIFTEEN

SHE WAS GOING to go to the ball.

If only because if she didn't Ed, her mother, the dressmaker and the Queen's assistants wouldn't forgive her.

The Queen had only returned to Florena briefly since her divorce had been announced. However, Ed wanted his mother to continue to be called the Queen, and to maintain a presence in Florena to support him if necessary.

Queen Isabella was not returning for the coronation. She had told Ed she didn't want to overshadow him. Simone suspected the real reason was that the Queen didn't want to see the former King Edouard, who would have to be at the coronation.

With the Queen so often away, her staff were at a loose end—and the thread they had latched on to was Simone. Simone was getting her hair and make-up done twice on the day of the coronation, which felt absurdly excessive.

'They want something to do. They *need* something to do,' her mother had insisted. 'They're helping me as well—and any of the other staff who would like their services.'

Simone carried the cardboard box back with her from the dress fitting. Her mother's old dress hadn't needed much work. The waist had been taken in and the bust taken out a little.

Her mother wouldn't tell her when or why she'd

bought the dress in the first place, but the whispers she'd heard between the Queen's assistants had been curious.

'It's not ready-to-wear. It's bespoke. Looks like the aesthetic from a decade ago,' they'd murmured.

That would make it too recent for it to be a dress Alea might have worn when she was dating Simone's father. What had her mother been doing ten years ago, wearing a designer dress much less owning one?

When Simone opened the door to the apartment her mother was pacing the room, but she smiled when Simone entered.

'Do you have time for a drink?' she asked. 'I feel like I've hardly seen you at all since you got back.'

Simone took a seat. Alea was right to heap guilt on her. She had been seeing Ed every spare moment he had—which meant she hadn't seen as much of her mother as either of them expected.

'I'm sorry, Mum.'

'There's no need to be sorry. I know you've been busy. I just thought it might be nice to have bit of time together. Catch up with no one else around. Do you have plans?'

Simone shook her head. Her mother knew she had been spending time with Ed, but if she realised that their relationship had changed she hadn't let on. Maybe that was the point of this conversation? Would she approve or caution Simone against it? She had no idea.

You're too suspicious. She just wants to spend some time with you.

'Wine?'

'Yes, please.'

Alea poured them both a glass and joined Simone by the fire.

'You've been spending a lot of time with Eddie, I understand?'

Ah. So this wasn't just a casual chat.

'He's my friend, and it's a stressful time for him.'

'I know that—and I'm not judging.'

Judging? The word hung between them. Her mother saying she wasn't judging felt very much like…judgement.

Her mother played with the stem of her wine glass for a long time.

She knows about Ed and me. She wants me to tell her.

But Simone didn't know what to tell her mother. She didn't know what was going on herself.

'You and Eddie have been friends for a long time,' said her mother, but I wonder if lately you've become closer?'

Simone dropped her head. She wasn't going to lie to her mother. 'I'm not really sure what's going on between us,' she confessed. 'It's new, and difficult, but for the time being we're taking it day by day.'

That was what she was telling herself as well. Taking each day as it came. Enjoying it while it lasted. Definitely not analysing her feelings in any depth at all.

'I'm not asking you to tell me, but I want you to know that you can.' Alea's voice was warm.

'Of course I know that I can, Mum. I can tell you anything.'

Alea reached over, took Simone's hand and squeezed it. 'That isn't what I wanted to talk about. I'm sorry this has come out all wrong...'

'Oh?' Simone was as confused as Alea looked.

'There's something I need to tell *you*,' her mother began. 'Something I never told you before.'

Alea's expression was pained, and Simone's mind instantly jumped to a million conclusions. Her mother was sick. Ed was sick...

'It's about the King. That is...the former King.'

Simone sat upright. Was King Edouard sick?

'It's about Edouard and I...'

It was funny how you could know something the second before you were actually told it.

Suddenly Simone just *knew*.

Was she a good guesser or was she simply remembering something she had forgotten from years ago?

Suddenly some of the cryptic things Ed had said in Paris became clear.

'You had an affair,' Simone said.

'You knew?'

Simone shook her head. 'Not until this second. Is it true?'

Alea nodded. 'Yes. Yes, we had an affair. You were a teenager, and your father had been gone a long while. Edouard is charming. You know that.'

Simone nodded. Like father, like son.

'And I was lonely and flattered. The King and Queen had ended their intimate relationship years before, and sometimes two people…'

Simone held up her hand. She was in shock, and surprised, but she wasn't angry. She was just processing.

'It's okay, Mum. I get it.'

There were many things that were not okay. The fact that the King had been cheating on his wife. The fact that her mother had kept this secret from her all this time. But she did understand that sometimes these things happened. And if the former King had been as hard to resist as his son, then Simone really didn't blame her mother.

'Did you love him?'

'No, I don't think so. But I was terribly fond of him and we had a lovely time. He made me feel good about myself.'

Simone grimaced. Why had her mother not felt good about herself?

'I knew there was no future in it, and I didn't want there to be one. Heavens, I didn't want him to leave the Queen! We tried our hardest to be discreet. But there is one thing I feel bad about. One regret.'

'The Queen?' Simone guessed.

'Isabella knew. She told Edouard that at least I

was age-appropriate and would be discreet.' Alea smiled, as if remembering something.

'The Queen knew?'

'Yes. It was all very adult.'

Simone wanted to be mature, but her stomach lurched at the thought of King Edouard—the philandering King—Alea and the Queen, all sharing this secret. The three of them might have been able to be calm about it, but Simone didn't think she would ever be able to treat such a situation in the same way the three of them seemed to have.

Perhaps she was just naive. Unsophisticated. Clueless.

'Why are you telling me now?' Simone asked, but she suspected she knew the answer. Ed had played a part in this.

'I regret agreeing to send you away to boarding school.'

'"Agreeing"? It wasn't your idea?'

'It was partly my idea. I did want you to get the best education you could. And I wanted you to have the opportunity to see life somewhere away from the palace. But it was Edouard who arranged it and paid for it. That is the part of the relationship I look back on with regret. It was only meant to be for a term or two. I thought you would come back. I always made it clear I wanted you to.'

It was as though her mother was telling her that the sky was green and always had been.

'I wasn't sent away because of the singing.' Her voice was soft.

'No. *No.* I can't believe you ever thought that.'

Simone had thought that the timing proved it. She'd made a fool of herself. She'd been asked if she wanted to go away and, feeling ashamed, she had agreed to go.

I was sixteen.

'It was to get me out of the way?'

'No, not as such… I thought it would be the best thing for your education. But I suppose that having you out of the palace may have been Edouard's intention.'

'I thought it was because of the singing… The video…' The contents of her stomach rose.

'I realise that now. And I'm sorry you thought you were being punished. That wasn't what it was about at all.'

'I wasn't in trouble?'

'Heavens, no, sweetheart. If I'd known how much that video had affected you I would never have sent you away to school to deal with it on your own. I'm so sorry.'

Simone took a sip of wine, but it tasted wrong in her mouth. 'Why didn't you tell me before?'

'I figured it was in the past.' Alea shrugged.

It was in the past.

The King had spectacularly moved on.

It was in the past for them—but Simone and Ed were still very much in the present.

And Ed knew. He had known all along.

The walls of the apartment closed in on her. Breathing became an effort.

They had all lied to her.

There was a lot to take in, and she couldn't do it here, in the warm apartment, with her mother looking on.

'I need a moment,' Simone said as she stood.

She had to get out.

She had to breathe.

'Simone, I had no idea the fallout from you singing that song had affected you so much. If I had I would have told you sooner.'

Simone nodded, but couldn't speak.

'Get some air. I'll be here when you get back if you want to talk some more.'

Alea looked stricken, but Simone couldn't worry about that now.

Everything she'd always believed had been turned on its head.

She grabbed her coat and left the apartment.

In summer the palace garden was the perfect place to sit and think. With its thick green grass, shady trees and a riot of coloured blooms, it was a calm oasis from the bustle and formalities of the palace. In winter it was the only place to go without actually leaving the palace walls.

The snow had stopped, but the cloud cover remained so the air was not frigid. Simone had on proper boots and a thick coat. She walked around the frozen pond to the small playground. She'd expected to find it dilapidated—it had been years since any children had lived permanently in the palace—but she was delighted to find it well maintained.

She brushed the snow off one of the swings and sat. It was smaller than she remembered, but she could still fit on the seat and gently swing.

It's not smaller...you're bigger.

Yeah? Well, memory was a fickle thing.

With one conversation half the things she remembered about her childhood had been flipped on their heads. Her mother? Ed's father?

What did that make her and Ed?

The sensible voice in her head said, *Nothing. It changes nothing between you and Ed.*

But another voice, the confused, lonely voice screamed, *Everyone knew but me. They let me think I was sent away because of the drama with the song.*

They had all let her down. Even Ed. Though as the dark settled in and her emotions stilled she realised he'd thought she already knew.

And, as upset as Simone was with her mother, she realised she was right. Alea was always asking her to come back. The first term at boarding school had been Alea's idea. But every term after that, and then Paris, had all been Simone's idea.

Even now she knew she would go back to Paris. Florena was not her home.

The evening wore on and the cold seeped into her fingers, but she wasn't going back inside. She didn't know these people any more. She didn't know her own mother.

Why had Alea had stayed working at the palace even after the affair was over? That didn't make much sense. Who would want to stay around to see their former lover every day once the affair was over?

'It was all very adult.'

Maybe she should just go back to Paris. It was her true home. Paris had never lied to her. She'd miss the coronation, but so what? Florena wasn't really her home. It hadn't been for years.

It was then that Ed found her, mentally booking her return flight to Charles de Gaulle.

'Hey,' he said gently, as if starting a conversation.

She had no time for niceties. 'You knew about the affair, didn't you?'

He took the swing next to her. 'Yes.'

'What I'm trying to understand is why she's told me now.'

'I asked her to,' he said simply.

Simone had guessed as much. 'Why?' she asked.

'Because I thought you needed to know. Not so much about the affair, but you needed to know why you were really sent to boarding school. It wasn't because of the singing or the video.'

'What on earth did you say to her?'

Oh, to have been a fly on the wall during that conversation…

He laughed. 'I was polite. So was she. I'm glad she understood where I was coming from.'

Simone rocked. The swinging was strangely calming.

'I felt bad that I knew and you didn't,' he said. 'But most of all I hate that you don't feel welcome here. I hate that you think you were banished.'

She could see his breath. He was wrapped up in a heavy coat and a thick grey scarf. His hair was slightly ruffled by the breeze. He looked as edible as ever.

Would there ever be a time when the sight of him didn't make her heart stop?

She might not have been banished because of the singing, but she'd still been sent away. They'd wanted to hide the affair from her.

'My mother and your father... Together.'

'My father and I have good taste in women. What can I say?'

'Stop! Ed, this changes everything. Between us.'

He got off his swing and stepped into her path, holding her swing still.

'No. It changes nothing between us. So what if our parents had an affair? It was ages ago. It's over.

She couldn't meet his eye. 'It changes the way I see my life. It changes things I thought about my-self.'

It was also mildly uncomfortable to know that their parents had once shared a bed. But it was more than that.

Simone's mother was palace staff. She might live in the palace, but she lived in the servants' apartments. Simone and her mother were the type of woman Kings had affairs with. Nothing more.

Yet you don't expect anything more from Ed. You don't want anything more. You don't want to be the Queen.

Her chest ached. She didn't want to be the Queen, but that didn't stop her wanting to be with Ed. And not as his mistress, but for ever. She'd tried to push those feelings aside, but they were overwhelming her. They were too strong to overcome.

Now, even in the crisp open air, she felt the world closing in on her again.

'Ed, I'm not sure I want to talk now. This is a lot to think about.'

I want to be with you. For ever.

'I understand, but please don't mind if I stay here, to make sure you don't die of exposure. Your mother said you've been out here for at least an hour. Can you still feel your feet?'

'I can neither confirm nor deny.'

'At least come in somewhere warm. You can pace the Great Hall if you want.'

'No, I can't; it's set up for the ball.'

She kept swinging.

Swing back, breathe in...swing forward, breathe out, she told herself.

They both swung back and forth for a while, but thankfully he swung in silence and let her process her thoughts.

'Did it go on for long?' she asked after a while.

'I don't know. A year, maybe.'

'Do you think they loved one another?'

'You'd have to ask her that.'

She had, and her mother had denied it.

'Do you think he loved her?'

Ed scoffed. 'You know my father. I don't think he's ever loved anyone.'

Alea understood what Simone's heart couldn't. Loving a king was hopeless.

She looked across at Ed. Swinging as if he was a kid again. He'd spoken to her mother, asked her to divulge her greatest secret, and done it in such a way as to get her to agree.

Ed really was a world-class diplomat. And he'd done it for her.

So she wouldn't think she'd been banished. So she might stay in Florena.

But for what? So she could remain his secret mistress? Simone loved Ed, but she was never going to agree to that.

'I still have to go back,' she told him. 'You know that.'

Ed paused and took a few swings before he replied. 'I would like you stay, but I understand that it's not simple.'

'Ed, I'm not going to stay here as your secret mistress. My mother might have been happy with that kind of arrangement, but—'

'Oh, Simone! No! That was not my intent. I don't want you to be my secret mistress,' he blurted.

'But that's all I'd ever be.' She picked up his hand. 'This week has been lovely, but we both know that's all it can be.'

For a brief moment she let herself hope that he would contradict her. Tell her that not only did he love her, but that he wanted to marry her. Despite his vow. Despite his country. Despite everything, he loved her and would love her for ever.

But he didn't say any of that. He simply said, 'If we only have a few more days we'd better make the most of it.'

She nodded. A few days. They had only that interlude before life would go back to normal.

Ed stood up and came to her swing, lifted her from it. His green eyes sparkled in the moonlight and he pulled her to him. His lips were warm and she leant into the kiss, but even as she did so he pulled back.

'Sim, you're freezing. Let's go inside.'

'I can't go in. You can keep me warm.' She tugged him closer.

'And have us both get frostbite? Do you want them to find our frozen corpses out here?'

Despite herself, she laughed. 'Think of the memes on that!'

He laughed too.

CHAPTER SIXTEEN

'YOUR FATHER WOULD like to talk to you,' Ed's assistant said.

Ed stood before the full-length mirror in his dressing room. The suit was itchy. Its fabric stiff and weighed down with medals and embellishments. Coronation outfits were definitely not made for lounging in on the couch. And he was still expected to get a cloak over this. Not to mention a five-pound crown on his head.

'Great. Please send him in,' Ed said, desperate for some pointers about how to get through today.

His assistant looked at his shoes. 'No, sir. He's on a video call at your desk.'

Ed's heart sank. His father should be at the palace by now, in time for the coronation.

He sat at his desk and opened the call. His father had a white wall behind him. He could've been anywhere in the world.

'Father, what's going on?'

His father smiled sadly. 'You're dressed. You look wonderful. Very regal.'

Despite his status, Ed felt himself blush. 'Thank you. Where are you?'

'That's what I wanted to talk to you about. I've decided not to come.'

Not come? This was the most important day of Ed's life—how could he not be there? It was obviously unorthodox for a former king to be at his successor's coronation, but they had talked about it and Ed had decided he wanted his father to be there. No matter how unusual it might be.

'How can you not be here? We agreed.'

'I know we did, but I've thought long and hard about it. I know how important it is to you—which is why I can't be there.'

Ed had never seen his father look so uncomfortable. So not regal.

He isn't the King any more. You are.

'It isn't right for a former king to be at the new King's coronation. As much as I want to support you, I think I will serve you best by giving you space. If I'm there the focus will be on me, and that wouldn't be fair to you. They need to see you as the one and only King.'

'But you're still my father—not my former father.'

'A coronation isn't a family affair. It's about you and the country.'

His father had never intended to come. He'd just agreed so that they wouldn't have this conversation until it was too late.

Now he'd have to do it all. The diplomacy. The outmanoeuvring of Laurent. Everything.

It hit him, almost as if for the first time, that his country's future was on his shoulders and his alone. He'd have to please and placate Laurent and his cronies on his own.

'We'd be stronger and more united together, not apart.'

'I can't leave Celine.'

Having his father at the coronation would be a good thing—having Celine there would most definitely not be. She was a lovely person, but if she was at the ceremony the media would have a field day.

'Not even for a couple of days?' he asked his father.

'Not even for a couple of days.'

Was he serious? His father had changed dramatically since meeting this woman.

Another thought occurred to Ed. 'Is she well? Is the baby okay?'

'Yes, she's well, and so is the baby.' His father smiled.

'Then why can't you leave her for a few days?'

'Because I don't want to.'

'I don't understand…'

'Because I love her.'

Ed laughed. 'Oh, don't be ridiculous.'

His father didn't know the meaning of the word.

'I'm not being ridiculous. I love her with all my heart.'

'Like you loved Mother? Like you loved Alea? Like you loved every other one of them?'

'I like your mother—don't get me wrong. And I adored Alea. But I didn't love them.'

Ed shook his head. 'You didn't even love Mother when you got married?'

'No—and I don't think she loved me either. It was a fortuitous, diplomatic and financial match. I tried to love her. I wish I had loved her. But I didn't. If I had, our lives would've been very different.'

'You would have been faithful, you mean?' Ed knew he sounded like a kid, and yet he was about to be crowned.

'Yes, that's exactly what I mean. I'm not proud of the way I've lived my life, but from now on things will be different.'

Ed scoffed. 'Yeah, right. I don't think the Berringer men are capable of love.'

Countless generations of men before them had proven the Berringer bloodline to be fickle and disloyal.

'I thought that too once, but I just hadn't met the right woman.'

'And you have now?'

Ed knew his voice was laced with sarcasm, but he didn't care. His father had let him down. *Again.* First, by abdicating without even a discussion and now by leaving him to get through this day alone.

'Yes. I was a little slow to the game, and my meeting with Celine was a little unusual. But I love her deeply, truly and for ever.'

For ever? How could he even know that?

'For ever? Seriously? You're a Florenan King. Not one of our ancestors has managed to stay with one woman.'

His father laughed. 'You've read too many fairy

tales. See them for what they are. Morality tales, at best. Propaganda from those in power, at worst. Laurent and his like use stories like that to their advantage.'

'Laurent didn't write the Florenan fairy tales. They've been around for years.'

'Yes. But he's using that story now, about the Cursed Kingdom, to try to persuade the people to get rid of us. It's a story. That's all. It has nothing to do with you.'

But Ed did know his family. His father. His uncle. His grandfather. And all who had come before them. He shook his head.

'Ed, son, you know as well as anyone that the stories the media tell about our family aren't true. Most of what they print about you is a lie. So why don't you see that story for what it is? A children's story. Marry the woman you love and you will not have any of the problems I had.'

His father ended the call shortly afterwards.

Ed stood and ran his hands through his hair, and squeezed his scalp for good measure. His father wasn't coming. His father was halfway across the world with his young girlfriend. He wasn't coming to the coronation—the most important day of Ed's life—because he wanted to be with her.

If he cared about you he wouldn't have got Celine pregnant in the first place.

If he truly cared for Ed he wouldn't have abdicated.

Objectively, from a public relations point of view, it did make sense for his father to stay away. But Ed had reasoned that having his father there would show the family was still united. And by seeming united they would appear stronger.

Although his father had a point as well. If he was there they would be sending a message to the world that his father was still around. It would look as if Ed was his father's puppet rather than his true successor.

If things had been different you wouldn't have expected your father to be at your coronation.

His death would have been the reason for his absence. But if things had been different Ed would probably have had many more years to prepare for this day. Not mere months.

No. He had to concede that his father had sound reasons for staying away. His absence was irritating, but it wasn't what was really bothering him. It wasn't the reason Ed wanted to run ten miles. Or scream until his lungs hurt. It wasn't the reason for this growing uncontrollable sensation in his chest.

He let out a cry and felt foolish. It was the other things his father had said. About Celine. About not wanting to leave her for a moment. About the fact that his father had never loved his mother.

'Marry someone you love and you won't have any of these problems.'

But how could he marry the woman he loved? It

wouldn't work. There were too many things keeping them apart.

The fact that he hadn't told her he loved her was just the first…

Simone had chosen her coronation day outfit in Paris. White and red—the Florenan national colours—it was a knee-length white shift dress paired with a red jacket and red pumps. Her hair was down, styled into gentle waves and completed with a small white hat.

Simone wasn't used to dressing so formally—long cardigans and floral dresses were her usual look—so she felt self-conscious when she stepped out of her room to find her mother.

Alea had also chosen white and red—a white suit and a red hat.

'You'll steal the show,' her mother said.

'I'm hoping to blend into the background.'

'As if you ever could. Besides, we're up front.'

Simone was horrified. 'At the cathedral?'

'Who else would be?'

'The Prime Minister, for starters. Other heads of state. All the important people!'

'We *are* the important people. Eddie has seated us with his close friends and family.'

'How do you know this?'

'He discussed the seating plan with me weeks ago. We're seated in the first row. Not in the centre—

that's reserved for his cousins and their families—but to one side.'

'How can we be at the front?'

On the screen. Photographed. Where her every move could be scrutinised. Her stomach rolled.

'What about the King?'

'If you mean the former King, I understand he hasn't returned.'

'What?

'It's hardly appropriate—'

'I need to speak to Ed.'

As soon as possible. He'd be devastated. When they'd spoken last night Ed had told her that the only good thing about the abdication would be his father being there to see his coronation.

Her mother gave her a quizzical look. 'Now?'

Simone didn't care what her mother thought. What any of them thought. This was between her and her best friend.

'Excuse me a moment.'

She went to her room and pressed Ed's number into her phone.

What was she thinking? He would be too busy preparing to get crowned to take her call.

But the phone clicked and he said in a whisper, 'Hello?'

'Ed, I just heard about your father.'

'Yeah, he called to tell me the good news.'

Simone heard muffled noises, a door closing, and

then Ed said, 'Dropped it on me when it was too late to do anything about it.'

'I'm so sorry.'

'Don't be. I see why. He can't be seen to be supporting me. His presence will detract from me and it should be my day. Former kings don't usually go to their successor's coronations.'

'Except as ghosts,' she said.

'Except as ghosts.' He laughed. 'I guess I just thought he would be there…and Mother too.'

It hit her. He really was alone now. Left by both his parents. That was why Simone and Alea were in the front row. She'd have to sit there now. For Ed.

'If it helps, I'm sure he'll be watching—and your mother too. I know they're both proud, even if they can't show it. And I am too,' she said.

'I hope you won't chicken out.' His voice was tinged with uncertainty.

'I wouldn't miss it. I'll be there with bells on.'

'Bells? Really? Don't ring them. That'll only draw attention to yourself.'

She laughed. 'I'd better let you go. See you out there. Good luck—and remember to take the crown, not the baseball hat.'

He laughed.

It was so strange, sitting in the front pew at Florena's royal cathedral. She'd been in the cathedral before, but it looked remarkably different now, decorated with red and white flags and banners interspersed with evergreen branches from Florena's famous pine trees.

The place was packed—literally to the rafters—with guests. Special seating had been erected for the occasion, to allow even more people to attend. But the ceremony itself was to be traditional and austere.

Ed had donated the money that would have been spent on processions and lavish feasts for the select few to charities in the city itself. Tonight's ball would be the only official celebration. Though the coronation would still show the world that Florena was as strong and independent as ever. So much more than a crown rested on Ed's head and shoulders. It was the fate of the whole country.

Simone no longer marvelled that she'd had an invitation. It seemed as though half the country was there. Though she did have literally a front row seat. Just below the high altar, so that when Ed walked in and took his position he was directly in front of her. Despite her earlier reservations, she knew she wouldn't have missed it for the world. Laurent and Morgane were on the opposite pew, but once Ed arrived they blurred into the background and all she saw was him.

He's the King. Your Ed is the King.

For as long as she lived it would be hard to explain her emotions that day. But there was one in particular that stayed with her, and that was the way her heart had felt as the crown had been placed on

Ed's head. He'd turned briefly to her, smiled and winked.

She'd resisted the urge to giggle, but her heart had never felt so full.

Because after everything he was still her Ed. And that realisation had been comforting and terrifying at the same time.

She'd hoped that maybe once the crown was on his head something would change. That *he* would change and become more distant and regal. She'd hoped that at the very least she would look at him differently. That it would make it easier for her to leave in two days' time.

But she still saw her Ed.

Only he wasn't her Ed any more.

He belonged to Florena now and would never belong to her.

After the ceremony was complete, and Ed had left the cathedral for photographs, Simone and Alea returned to their apartment to get ready for the ball.

'Stay.'

She sat on her bed with the silk of her dress spread out around her and put on her shoes.

What if she could do what Ed suggested and rise above her fears and stay? Learn to drown out the noise from the trolls? Trust that Ed and the palace would be able to shield her?

She had sat in the front row at his coronation and

she had felt fine. More than that, she wouldn't have missed seeing that special moment for anything.

She'd miss out on so many experiences with Ed if she returned to Paris.

Wasn't he worth it?

Yes, but it wasn't that simple. She had a life in Paris, and she wasn't about to give that up to skulk around the palace with Ed until their affair ran its course.

Because it would. Ed wasn't going to marry—her or anyone else—so a secret affair was all it ever could be.

There was a knock at her bedroom door.

'Is everything all right?' asked her mother. 'We'll be late.'

Simone took a deep breath and emerged from her room. Alea brushed a tear from her eyes and sniffed another away.

'I knew that dress would look wonderful on you. You look spectacular.'

She carried her mother's compliment like a shield as they walked across the palace to the great hall. Did she imagine it or was everyone looking at her? It was probably because she was self-conscious, wearing such a magnificent dress. When she climbed the grand staircase up to the ballroom, she had to lift the voluminous skirt so she didn't trip.

Yeah, that would make a great photo. Her falling face-down on the palace stairs tangled in her dress.

But Simone made it to the top of the stairs without incident and more people turned. She walked through the doors. No, she wasn't imagining it. People *were* turning to look at her—but they weren't laughing. They were smiling.

Still, Simone's heart hammered behind the corset of the dress as she and Alea walked along the short receiving line.

She recognised Ed's closest relatives, his cousins the Dukes of Linden and Clichy, accompanied by their wives. And after them stood Ed. He was shaking someone's hand as Simone approached, but he stopped, paused for far too long.

Simone felt heat rise in her cheeks, but she focused on the two dukes. They greeted her warmly, though showed no sign of knowing who she was. There was no reason why they should, she reminded herself. They'd only met her as children. The last time she'd seen either of them had been Ed's seventeenth birthday, and they clearly wouldn't connect her to the teenager who had embarrassed herself in front of the world.

Maybe no one else would either.

Then she reached Ed. He kissed her mother on both cheeks first, and then swallowed hard. Simone was next. She held out her hand and curtsied, knees wobbling, unused to executing the movement in high heels. Once she'd risen he pulled her in for a kiss on the cheek, just like he had her mother. Only on the second kiss he held her shoulders and kept her close.

'Not only are you the most beautiful woman here tonight,' he whispered. 'But you're also the most beautiful woman I've seen in my entire life. If you dance with anyone else I think I'm going to have them sent to the dungeon.'

She laughed. 'Do you even have a dungeon?'

'I'm not sure. Just…' He pulled her close again. 'Please, save a dance for me.'

Simone floated into the ballroom.

CHAPTER SEVENTEEN

IF THEY HAD handed out dance cards Simone's would have been full. Particularly after Ed had singled her out for the second dance, after his obligatory one with the highest-ranking woman at the ball, the Duchess of Linden.

Simone had been worried she'd be standing next to her mother all night, like a spare part, as her mother spoke to her colleagues and friends, but Simone had met many people. Women she didn't know had come up to her and asked about her dress, and men had asked her to dance. They'd all been friendly and not at all intrusive. Conversation had come easily. Particularly when she'd divulged that she had grown up in the palace and now lived in Paris. People found her life story delightful and asked about her bookshop.

Not one of them thought she didn't deserve to be there.

Not one of them recognised her as the hashtag *palaceserenade* girl.

Later in the night, when her feet ached, she went to find her mother. She sat and reacquainted herself with some of the palace staff, past and present, whom she hadn't seen in years.

Then she and Ed snatched a brief moment together, as she was on her way to the bathroom. They stood, respectably apart, and spoke briefly.

'Thank you for coming,' he said.

'Of course.'

'Not just for tonight. Thank you for being here this week. I don't know what I'd have done without you. I couldn't have got through today without you here.'

She smiled at him, unsure of what to say. She wanted to reach over and hug him, but knew that was out of the question with everyone looking on.

'If it were up to me I'd just dance with you all night,' he whispered.

'But you have to mingle.'

'I do have to mingle, and I fear that if I keep dancing with you then more than one person is bound to notice that I can't keep my eyes off you.'

Simone's body came alive at his words, and she wanted to slip her arms around him and press her body against his. But she knew he was right, so they parted. Ed brushed his hand against hers, sending sparks right up her arm. Two hands touching had never felt so exciting. She turned quickly, so no one would notice the blush in her cheeks.

She glimpsed Laurent and Morgane once or twice, but they didn't come close to where she was. She felt surrounded and protected by friendly people all night long.

When it was all over she and her mother returned, exhausted, to their apartment. Alea helped her undress and Simone went to the bathroom to wash off the make-up and brush out the styling.

She had survived the ball! Not only that—she had thrived. Her mind was dizzy with thoughts of the evening. She'd laughed and talked with so many interesting people. None of whom had thought she was out of place.

She heard soft voices and when she emerged in her pyjamas she saw Ed, standing in the living room. Like her, he'd changed out of his stiff uniform and formal clothes, and was wearing grey track pants and a soft blue sweater. Her fingers itched to stroke him.

'I'll bid you both good evening. Or is it good morning?' Alea said, leaving them alone.

He came straight to her and wrapped her in his arms.

'Should you be here?' she asked.

'It's my palace now.'

She swatted him. 'Here? Now?'

'Do you want me to leave?'

'Of course not.' They only had two more nights together. 'But my mother—'

'Knows you've been sneaking out to my apartment.'

Simone had suspected as much, and found she didn't mind her mother knowing about her and Ed. After all, if she ever needed to go to someone for advice about navigating a secret affair with a king she could think of no better person.

'I just want to hold you,' he said. 'I've never been so exhausted in my life and I just want to be with you.'

They fell into her bed and held one another. With her last ounce of energy she picked up his hand and entwined her fingers with his.

'Do you feel different?' she asked.

'I think maybe I do. But that isn't because of my new hat. I think it's because I now feel that my father really has left.'

Oh, Ed.

'But I realised something today. I'm actually lucky. I could've become King at any moment if he had passed away. But I'm lucky because I can still go to him for advice. He isn't dead. Just living somewhere else. Not many kings are that lucky.'

'I'd say hardly any at all,' Simone said.

'I just have a new job. And it's a job that I've been trained for. It's a job I think I can do.'

She squeezed him. 'I'm really glad to hear that.'

'But it's a job that would be much easier if I had someone else here with me.'

'Your mother?'

'No, Sim. You.'

'Oh, Ed. We've talked about this.'

'But have we really? We've skirted around it, but we've never really talked about it.'

They had, hadn't they? He wasn't going to marry anyone and she wasn't moving back here.

'What would happen?' she asked softly.

'You would move back here and be my girlfriend.'

Did kings even have girlfriends? And was that enough? Was a title and a ring important to her? Maybe not. They were Simone and Ed. Maybe it didn't matter what anyone called them or how their relationship was defined. Because they would always be Simone and Ed. Best friends. And nothing, no one in the world, could change that.

You'd have to move back to Florena.

For the first time she didn't panic at the thought. People had been so friendly and welcoming to her tonight. She'd had a marvellous time.

What was more, after Alea's revelation she understood that she hadn't been sent away to boarding school because she was an embarrassment, someone to be banished from Florena, but because of something that had nothing to do with her at all.

The people didn't think she was a disgrace.

Some of her own fears began to dissolve. Maybe she could start by returning to Florena more often and see how that went? And surely Ed would have to make some diplomatic trips to Paris?

'What would I do?' she asked. 'I couldn't work.'

'You could if you wanted to. You could do anything you want. I'd see to it. I am the King.'

Was he right? Or was he daydreaming?

'Do we have to decide now?'

Exhaustion was overwhelming her. Pushing her lids over her eyes. Maybe she could stay…? Maybe her fears were all unfounded…?

'No, we don't. I just want you to know that I want to be with you.'

Simone fell asleep in his arms and knew that.

Simone laughed, glowed, and looked as though she was having a wonderful time. He loved seeing her like this. Not just enjoying herself, but relaxed and thriving at the ball.

He tried to go her, but someone stopped him. He was stuck, listening to a boring conversation about the crown jewels.

He finally extricated himself as politely as he could, took two steps, but Laurent blocked his way.

Simone disappeared into the crowd. He pushed after her, but again his way was blocked—this time by two men who looked like Laurent.

He caught a glimpse of silver in the next room, but knew he could never reach her. She kept slipping further and further away...

Ed woke up drenched in sweat and shaking.

Simone had not slipped away. She lay next to him now, still fast asleep. Her golden hair was spread around her on the pillow. She looked so peaceful he had to stop himself leaning over and pressing his lips to her cheek in case he woke her.

It was still dark, but a glance at his watch told him it was after six and the palace would soon be waking. He should get back to his apartment as quickly as he could. He trusted his staff, but rumours had a way of leaking out, and the last thing he wanted was any undue attention being drawn to Simone. He could handle any bad press about himself—after yesterday he somehow felt more confident that he could beat Laurent at that game—but if Simone was spooked by internet trolls again she might never return.

As he walked back to his apartments he thought about which rooms were empty and where Simone might be comfortable. Somewhere as close as possible to him. Maybe she could visit more often, or even divide her time between here and Paris. If she was going to do that she'd need her own space.

And then what?

The palace looked different this morning. The sun was slowly rising, and though he had already been King for three months, his being crowned officially had shifted something. Now his father really couldn't come back.

He'd meant what he'd said to Simone last night. He had made his peace with his new position and yesterday had been invigorating. He was going to be the best King Florena had ever had. He would make the Florenans proud of their country and its independence and make sure they put any idea of a union with France behind them as soon as possible.

'If you marry the woman you love then it will all be okay.'

His father was a lovesick fool, and probably rewriting history. He was sure his parents had loved one another once. Even if only for a short time.

What Ed and Simone had was stronger than anything his forebears had felt. Ed and Simone were old friends. Best friends. And amazing together in bed. Surely the odds of a long and happy relationship were stacked in their favour?

As he approached his apartments a staff member

passed him and gave him a knowing wink. Why would the King be entering his apartments at six a.m. unless he hadn't slept there all night?

But what if Ed was just as weak as his father? What if he was the unreliable player everyone said he was?

The Playboy Prince? No. He had to block out those voices. They did not speak the truth. He wasn't a playboy. Or a womaniser, like the tabloids said. He was just Ed. A regular guy. Simone Auclair's best friend.

He couldn't imagine cheating on Simone. But if what one day, after those first heady days disappeared, that changed? What if he was as fickle as his father? And his grandfather? And every other King Edouard who had come before him?

What if he played right into Laurent's hands and showed him that the royal family was the disgrace he'd said they were?

He pushed open the door to his rooms.

No. He had to get Laurent out of his head. He would never cheat on Simone. She was his best friend. The person he felt closest to in the entire world.

In his suite, breakfast was laid out for him, and his valet stood by the table, holding the newspapers.

'Sir, there is something you need to see.'

Ed took one look at the front pages and knew that today was not going to go as planned. There was no way Simone would agree to stay now. She'd probably get on the first plane back to Paris.

CHAPTER EIGHTEEN

IT WAS LATE when Simone emerged from her room. Ed had left early. She hadn't expected him to stay. It was another work day for him. So she was surprised to see him in the kitchen, talking to her mother. He was wearing a suit and tie and she stopped. He looked handsome, but she decided she much preferred him wearing nothing at all.

They both turned to look at her when she entered.

'Don't you have a country to run? To save?'

She smiled as she said it, so he'd know she was joking. The truth was she was delighted to wake up and see her two most favourite people in the world.

Neither smiled back.

'Sim, darling, sit down. I'll get you a coffee.'

This wasn't good.

'What's the matter?' she asked as she pulled out a chair, her legs suddenly unsteady.

Ed sat next to her. 'There's been some media coverage.'

She pulled a face. Of course there was media coverage. It had been his coronation.

'Of you?'

They both shook their heads and it hit her.

'Oh… Me?'

But she hadn't done anything! She'd been one of hundreds of guests at the coronation. She and Ed had only danced once, as they had planned, and had only spoken to one another that brief time. They had been so careful not to do or say anything too intimate, in case they were filmed or overheard. Besides, everyone had liked her! No one had recognised her or known she was in that video.

'Can I see?'

Ed and his mother conferred with a look, and then Ed slid an open tablet across the table to her.

The King and the Crooner was the headline, and below it was a photo of the two of them dancing. But Simone's focus was immediately drawn to the next image. A still of the video taken at Ed's seventeenth birthday party.

Bile rose in her empty stomach and she scrolled down to the article itself.

Back to embarrass the Crown: the servant's daughter who managed to manipulate her way into the coronation and the celebratory ball. It seems Simone Auclair won't give up her ambitions with the King.

Simone even managed to trap the King into a dance. But we all know the newly crowned King is vulnerable to a pretty girl. It's no secret that he's known all over the world as the Playboy Prince.

Our sources tell us she is currently running a dusty bookshop in Paris, and it is still unclear how or why she managed to connive her way back into the palace after causing so much disgrace fourteen years ago.

A spokesperson from the Prime Minister's department has said they are looking into the matter and assessing any security risks.'

'Wow... This is...'

'Lies,' Ed said.

How did they know all this stuff? Only someone who knew her would be able to spin it this way.

'Yes, but not entirely. There's just enough truth in it, isn't there? That's what so awful. It isn't lies. Half-truths, maybe. But I *am* the daughter of a member of palace staff. I *do* run a dusty bookshop. I *have* been hiding in Paris.'

Simone opened up her own social media. She kept it very private, and her settings were as secure as they could be. She didn't even use her own name, for crying out loud, but went by *BookGirl*.

And yet there were many messages about the coronation and the ball. And they were all vile.

Her eyes went to a particular person.

MAL17. The thumbnail was an avatar, different from last time, but the words were similar.

Bad singer, bad dancer...why hasn't she died from embarrassment?

Her hand shook and Ed took the phone from her. He frowned.

'*MAL17.* That was one of the trolls from before,' she said.

The one who had told her to die.

'From when? The video?'

'Yes. I recognise the name. Or rather I recognise the comments. The words are the same. This is the same person.'

'I'll get Home Affairs to look into it.'

Home Affairs. The government.

If they couldn't trust Laurent, they couldn't trust his government. Ed was only a figurehead. He didn't control the government. Laurent did.

She felt even more exposed.

'No. Not them.'

'Why not?'

'Because…because Laurent is after you. Is there someone else you can ask?'

'Laurent wouldn't risk getting involved in something like this. It's too tawdry. Surely it's beneath him?'

'By attacking me he's attacking you. It sounds like his *modus operandi*.'

Ed and his mother shared a look. They thought she was overreacting.

Maybe it wasn't Laurent. But she knew who else it might be. And once it occurred to her she wondered why she hadn't realised it before. It was so obvious.

'Morgane. His girlfriend. Morgane Lavigne.'

She saw their faces turn from incredulity to understanding.

'It's a long shot… Would she risk it?'

'*MAL*. Morgane Lavigne. I bet her middle name begins with an A.'

Ed and her mother were staring at her with open mouths.

'Oh, God. Am I paranoid? It sounds crazy when I say it aloud.'

'You're not crazy or paranoid. You've been viciously and unfairly attacked.'

'Do you want me to go back to Paris?' she said.

'No!' they shouted in unison.

She didn't want to be here, but even Paris might not be the sanctuary she thought it was. If this *MAL17* knew about her bookshop then she might be followed there.

She shivered. Where could she go? Canada? Australia? The middle of the Pacific Ocean wouldn't be far enough.

'Let's look at it before you go anywhere,' said Ed.

She opened a browser on her phone and typed 'Morgane Lavigne' into the search engine. The page opened with lots of glamorous shots of Morgane with Laurent, and also some from years ago, with Ed. Simone swallowed down bile and clicked on one of the links.

Morgane Adrianna Lavigne.

She passed it to Ed.

'I might be paranoid. I might be wrong. But I have this feeling…'

Ed nodded, and then pulled her into an embrace. He held her as if he was trying to protect her and give her strength all at once. She appreciated it, but knew that even he couldn't protect her completely.

No one could.

'I'll get someone to look into it.'

'But not anyone connected to Laurent. Promise?'

'I promise.'

He kissed her on the forehead and left.

'I hope you're right,' said Alea, passing her a coffee and a plate of warm pastries.

'Why?'

'If it's her they'll expose her. It'll all be over.'

Simone shook her head. 'I don't think it will ever be over. I know these things go on and on. She's just one of many.'

'But she's not a nobody. She knows the royal family and she's dating Laurent. She isn't a random person.'

Alea gripped Simone's hand. She started to speak again and then stopped.

Finally, just as Simone was losing sensation in her hand, her mother said, 'Simone, I'm so sorry again you had to deal with all this alone last time. I had no idea.'

Simone nodded. She had forgiven her mother. It was no one's fault except the internet trolls'. 'I know Mum. I know.'

'Can I cook you something?'

Simone couldn't drink the coffee, let alone eat

anything. 'I think I want to go back to bed for a while. It was a late night.'

'Do you want to talk?'

Alea's eyes pleaded with her. But Simone didn't want to talk. She didn't want to be awake.

She shook her head. 'I just want to bury myself in my bed.'

And she did.

Simone woke a few hours later, not at all refreshed, and feeling just as beaten as she'd felt earlier that morning.

It was just like last time.

She'd been in this same room. The same bed. Looking at the same snowy view out of her window.

It was as though she'd been transported back fourteen years.

Nothing had changed. Including her sense of suffocation and the desire to get out of there.

Her flight wasn't until tomorrow, but that was less than twenty-four hours to go, and she had no intention of leaving the apartment. She still wasn't hungry, but her mouth was parched. She went to get a glass of water, but as she entered the kitchen Alea sat up, alert and concerned.

'Did you sleep?'

'A little.'

'Do you feel better?'

Simone frowned. 'I think I will when I get back to Paris.'

'Oh, Sim. No. Please at least stay and see how this all plays out.'

'There's no point. No matter what happens, I have to leave.'

'But why? If they find out who spoke to the paper... If they find out who wrote those things...'

'That won't change anything. Not really. Another troll will pop up in their place. You know that. And they will always dig up that video.'

Alea brewed new coffee and this time Simone accepted it, and curled up on the couch.

'The sooner I get back to Paris the sooner I'll be able to get away from all this embarrassment.'

'Why are you embarrassed?' Alea asked. 'You've done nothing wrong.'

But she knew she must have. Half the world was saying so.

'Mum, the comments are horrible. Some of them are telling me to die.'

Alea picked up her hand and squeezed. 'The comments *are* awful. Inexcusable. Criminal. But Eddie is getting someone to look into them.'

Simone nodded. She was out of words. She knew that no matter what Ed found these people would continue. Trolls always found a way. Being in the spotlight made you a target.

Alea scratched her head. 'How does Eddie do it, I wonder?'

'Ed? He was born into it.'

Ed didn't love the scrutiny, but he knew it was part and parcel of the job.

Simone sighed. 'He has a thick skin. He doesn't let things get to him.'

'Doesn't he?'

It wasn't a rhetorical question. Alea put her hands on her hips, as though waiting for Simone to think carefully about her answer.

'I don't know what I would have done without you.'

'I couldn't have got through today without you there.'

They weren't just the platitudes Simone had assumed them to be. Ed managed because he had supportive friends and colleagues around him. When the video of her singing had gone viral Simone had been alone. She'd had no one to help her deal with it. They had sent her away. Maybe things would have been easier if she hadn't had to go through it by herself.

'It does bother him, but he draws strength from the people he loves. Including you,' Alea said, echoing her daughter's thoughts.

Simone nodded. Then shook her head. 'I don't think I'm strong enough.'

'But you wouldn't be alone. You would have me. And Ed.'

'Oh, Mum, if I stay here it'll get worse. And if the government gets wind of the fact that Ed and I are more than friends then they'll use it as more ammunition. *The Playboy Prince strikes again.* I couldn't do that to him.'

'Then here's a crazy idea… Why don't you marry him?'

Simone nearly spat out the last of her coffee. 'He's not going to marry me.'

'Why not?'

'Because he's Ed. He doesn't believe in marriage. He's the Playboy Prince.'

Alea laughed. 'You know him. You know that's all nonsense, don't you? It's all made up by the press. Eddie hasn't slept with any more women than the average thirty-year-old.'

'How do you know?'

'Because I know Eddie. I live here. I see him. I know that pictures of him with pretty women sell papers. I know most of what's published in the press is lies.'

That was what Ed had said the other day, wasn't it? He hadn't slept with even a fraction of the women everyone thought he had.

But it was more than that. 'He's too worried about Florena. He thinks if he doesn't marry then there won't be any further scandal. He thinks not getting married is the way to save the royal family's reputation.'

Alea laughed. 'Really? That's nonsense. Being married—to the right woman—would do wonders for his reputation. And for the monarchy. Who doesn't love a royal wedding?'

'Everyone loves a royal wedding…until the inevitable royal divorce.'

Alea frowned. 'Oh, you two are impossible. What makes you think you and Eddie wouldn't last the distance? You do love him, don't you?'

Don't fall. Don't fall.

'He's my oldest friend.'

Alea raised an eyebrow. 'Sounds like a pretty good foundation for a marriage.'

'Ed hasn't asked me—and he won't.'

It was a ridiculous idea. Besides, she could never be with him. Being married to the King would draw even more trolls in her direction and make things worse than they already were.

Simone went back to bed. Just like last time, sleep was the only thing that stopped the thoughts in her head. Though she never stayed asleep for long.

The next time she woke it was nearly dark outside. She pulled on her dressing gown and went into the living room. Alea was sitting by the fire, still looking concerned.

'How are you doing?' she asked.

Simone shrugged.

'Eddie called while you were sleeping, but he asked me not to wake you. He has some meetings, and an official dinner, but said he will come by once he's finished.'

Simone longed to see him, but at the same time she knew it was the last thing either of them needed.

'He said to tell you he's working on it. He seems to think that your theory about Morgane may not be out of left field.'

Simone sighed. She should be happy to be right, but she wasn't. Knowing who it was didn't make it any easier to accept.

'I wouldn't be at all surprised if she was behind the video of Eddie's birthday party too.'

'Why on earth would she do such a thing? Why film me and then post it?'

'Because she was jealous.'

'Of me? Why? She was the one he was with at the birthday party.'

Simone could still remember how close Ed and Morgane had been. Their legs tangled in one another's on a sofa.

'Because Eddie loves you.'

Simone grimaced. 'He doesn't. And he certainly didn't then.'

'Oh, Simone. He always has. You're the love of his life. His best friend. He's always loved you. Just for a while he was too young to realise.'

Alea put an old movie on the TV and left Simone staring blankly at it while she prepared some food in the kitchen. A hearty chicken soup with fresh bread. Simone didn't feel like eating, but when the smell hit her she began to salivate.

They ate slowly in front of the television.

'Mum, where did you get that dress? The one I wore last night?'

'I was wondering when you would ask that. Edouard gave it to me.'

That made sense.

'When did you wear it?'

'I didn't.'

'Then why did he give it to you?'

'He wanted me to accompany him to a dinner. I thought about it, but refused. It wouldn't have been right.'

'So you broke up with him?'

'I suppose so. But these things are rarely one-sided. We couldn't give each other what the other needed.'

'Just like Ed and I.'

'No, Simone, not like that at all. You and Eddie are very different. You could find a way through if you wanted to.'

But her mother was wrong. There was no path forward for her and Ed, just as there had been none for Alea and Edouard.

Ed didn't love her. And even if he did he wasn't going to risk his country's future for her.

Besides, she'd never let him.

CHAPTER NINETEEN

As soon as he'd cancelled his remaining appointments for the evening, Ed pulled off his tie and exited his office by the back door. He knew the quickest route to the apartment above the kitchens and took it, finding himself unable to stop smiling at every single person he passed.

He'd decided.

He laughed when he thought of how it had taken him so long when it was really the simplest and most natural thing in the world.

Alea let him in. Simone was reclining on the couch, tousled and gorgeous.

She sat up quickly when she saw him. 'I thought you had a dinner.'

Ed walked in slowly. He was suddenly more nervous now than he'd been entering the cathedral yesterday.

'I cancelled it. I had something more important to do.'

'What?'

'Talk to you.'

Alea cleared her throat. 'I have plans to meet a friend this evening. Have a good night.'

Simone looked at her mother, watching her leave. They both knew Alea had no such plans.

Ed glanced at the other armchairs, but chose the sofa, where Simone was ensconced in a pile of blankets. Guilt tightened around his heart. She wouldn't have to go through this again. He'd make sure of it. No matter how long it took, he would find out who was behind these attacks on her and make it stop.

Simone cleared away the blankets and he sat next to her. He moved to pick up one of her hands, but she put both in her lap before he could.

'I came as soon as I could,' he said.

'It's okay. You're busy. You didn't have to come.'

'Of course I did.'

'Mum said you might be able to trace the article to Morgane?'

'Possibly. We may not know for a few days. Would you…? Simone, why don't you stay until we know?'

She looked down and his heart crashed.

'I have to go back to Paris. My life is there.'

'What if your life was here? Your mother's here. And I'm here,' he said slowly, cautiously.

He had once thought that he would never marry, because marriage had only brought unhappiness and scandal to his family. But now he had figured out the way to stop that. The way to stop scandal wasn't to avoid marriage. It wasn't to avoid commitment. The way to avoid scandal was to make sure you married the right person and committed to them totally. Completely. And the right person—the only person—was sitting right next to him.

'I love you, Simone.'

She swallowed. 'I know you do. We're friends.'

'No. Not as a friend, but as my lover, my soulmate, my life partner. I love you in every sense of the word—body and soul. You are my match. And I want you to be my queen.'

She tilted her face back and closed her eyes. She drew in a deep breath and said, 'Love doesn't last. You said that.'

'That was before I knew what it was,' he said softly.

She shook her head. 'I know how you feel about marriage. I know that it's the last thing you want.'

'No. I've changed my mind. It was after I spoke to my father yesterday, actually. I've realised that the best way to avoid scandal is to marry the right woman. Marry the woman I love. Hiding from commitment won't help.'

Simone opened her eyes and faced him. 'I wish I could believe you.'

His heart thudded to the floor. He dragged both hands through his hair, gripping his skull. 'Why can't you?'

'You just said you want to marry me to avoid scandal. After everything you've told me, that doesn't make any sense.'

'Of course it makes sense! I love you. I'd never cheat on you. I'd never leave you.'

'It's been less than a week. Our relationship has barely begun.'

'It hasn't been a week. It's been a lifetime! I know you and you know me.'

Simone raised one perfect eyebrow and shook

her head. 'I don't know that I do. Four months ago we sat by the Seine and you told me that you would never marry. That love didn't exist. And now you want me to upend my entire life? Ed, I care for you deeply. But this isn't the way to get me to stay here for longer.'

Why was she arguing?

Why didn't she believe him?

Because you've spent your entire life telling her you don't believe in marriage. You've spent your entire life actively avoiding marriage.

'Don't you…?'

At the last moment he thought better of asking the question.

Don't you love me too?

She'd loved him once. Loved him enough to stand up in front of everyone he knew and sing to him.

No. She had a crush on you when she was sixteen. Like every other girl her age in the country at the time. She's smart enough to know that the fantasy of dating a prince is far removed from the reality of marrying a king.

He wasn't Ed, telling Simone that he loved her. He was a king, asking the woman he loved to turn her life upside down for him. Simone was spooked by the press and not without reason. She hated the spotlight. He'd been a fool to ever think she'd say yes.

It felt as though his five-hundred-year-old palace was crumbling around him. Everything he'd ever told himself had been wrong. Everything he believed his whole life had been wrong. And now he was adrift. Alone.

'No. Never mind.'

He shook his head. It didn't matter. Even if a part of her did love him, it wasn't fair of him to ask her what he was asking.

Duty would be his to fulfil alone.

I love you.'

He'd said it. And Ed didn't lie to her.

He loved her as a friend…but big love? Everlasting love?

He'd told her that didn't exist.

'I'll go. I'm sorry.'

He stood and walked to the door.

Simone moved to get up from the sofa, but he waved her back.

'Ed, I'm sorry…'

'Don't be.'

He shook his head, but wouldn't meet her eyes. Was he crying?

No. He couldn't be.

And he was out through the door before she could reach him.

I love you.'

The floor felt unsteady. But that was probably just her entire reality being tipped upside down. And shaken for good measure.

'I love you.'

She'd made the right decision.

The last thing Ed needed—the last thing the country needed—was someone like her in a relationship with the King. Rightly or wrongly, she brought controversy with her. Ed's main focus needed to be on improving the reputation of the monarchy, not defending her. She was a liability.

Ed's scheme to get married to avoid scandal was so bizarre that he'd wake up tomorrow and change his mind. He was panicked. Not thinking straight. That was all.

Because why would he want to marry her?

He loves you.

And you love him.

Simone buried her face in her hands. Of course she loved him! She'd never stopped. Not since that fourteen-year-old boy had arrived home from school that summer with broad shoulders and a whole new foot of height.

She'd loved him when she'd sung to him at his seventeenth birthday party. Promising that she'd always love him.

And she'd loved him when he'd arrived on her doorstep in Paris. And when they'd kissed by the Seine. She'd loved him then and she would always love him.

In fact, she loved him too much to tell him how much she loved him.

She loved him, she wanted him, she needed him to breathe.

I ache for you. I adore you. I yearn for you.

But it didn't matter what she felt. Love wasn't always enough, and she had to start protecting her heart.

Simone's phone pinged and she picked up her phone from where she had thrown it earlier. There was a message from Julia. She opened it, but her chest constricted when she saw that Julia had sent a photo from the ball. The one from the article Ed had showed her earlier.

OMG you two are adorable. This pic has made my heart melt! xo

Simone enlarged the photo on her screen and studied it properly.

The photo wasn't bad—that was part of the problem. They both looked lovely. They really did look adorable. She studied the way Ed was looking at her in a way that was impossible to do when he was actually looking at her. His eyes were soft. The skin around them creased. Any outsider who looked at this photo would know that the two of them were very much into one another.

They had both tried not to be obvious. Tried to be discreet all evening. But the photographer had managed to capture a moment between them when their gazes had been locked and slightly dreamy. It had just been one moment, she remembered, but it had been enough.

Was that how the world saw her?

Her hand shook as she opened her social media.

She was tagged in so many posts she couldn't count them. A quick glance showed her that while many were telling her how lovely she looked, most were less complimentary. They called her an upstart. A gold-digger. Ugly. Fat.

She threw her phone on to the couch and clutched a pillow.

If she stayed in Florena…if she stayed with Ed… it would always be like this.

She could ignore social media. She could stop reading the papers. But she couldn't divorce herself from reality entirely.

Even if Morgane turned out to be this particular troll and could be stopped, others would pop up in her place. The palace could protect her to some extent, but it was still up to her. Was she strong enough?

And then she did something she hadn't done in years. She clicked on the link to the video of her singing at Ed's seventeenth birthday party. Her hands trembled.

The opening bars of the song played and her muscles gave the familiar involuntary reaction they always did when she heard them. But this time the rest of the song was unfamiliar. Because *she* was singing.

She was so young…but also so beautiful and sweet. Why had no one told her how gorgeous she was?

She wanted to reach into the screen and shake that sixteen-year-old, tell her how beautiful she was. She was wobbly on her high heels, and she kept tugging at her dress, but her face was gorgeous. Young and bright and hopeful. Untouched by worry and strain.

There was also nothing particularly bad about her singing. She wasn't ever going to win a recording contract, but she held the tune.

She hadn't made a fool of herself. Not really.

No one should have posted that video. No one should even have been taking photos at that party. It had been in the palace, and the guests had all signed non-disclosure agreements.

She should have been safe.

None of this was her fault.

It was someone else's.

And the article published this morning had been lies.

She'd believed the trolls. She didn't blame herself for that. She'd been a teenager and all alone.

But not once had Simone done anything wrong or embarrassing.

And even if she had that was still no reason to attack someone on social media.

She wasn't being weak by leaving. She was being strong. She was leaving the man she loved because it was for the best. She was being strong for him, and she had to keep being strong.

She flicked through the posts until she finally fell asleep on the couch.

Ed would have been lying if he'd said that sitting across the desk watching Pierre Laurent sign his resignation letter wasn't deeply, deeply satisfying. A caretaker Prime Minister had been appointed, and would form a new government as soon as possible.

Ed understood that Laurent and Morgane planned to leave the country later that day. Their reputations were irretrievably ruined in Florena. But he hoped they wouldn't inflict themselves upon another unsuspecting nation.

Laurent looked at him and smirked as he pushed the paper across Ed's desk. Ed smiled back broadly and honestly.

Good riddance.

It turned out the French government had been keeping a close eye on Laurent for a while, given his declared ambitions. They had traced a lot of unusual social media activity to Morgane's PR firm. Simone was not their only victim. Morgane's firm had created a network of fake accounts to attack all kinds of people—especially Laurent's political opponents.

After that it hadn't taken long to also determine that Morgane was the source of the leaked video from Ed's seventeenth birthday party.

The fact that the PM and his girlfriend's private PR firm were leaking material to the press and running so many private social media accounts had caused the newspapers to publish many follow-up articles, and Laurent's resignation had come faster than anyone had guessed it would after his cabinet told him he had lost their confidence.

Laurent might be gone, but it was two days too late. If Ed had done something about Simone's trolls earlier he might have stopped this latest attack on her. Simone might have agreed to stay.

Now…? Now there was no way. How could he convince her to embark on a public life with him when he knew as well as she did that he'd failed to protect her? And there was no guarantee he'd be able to stop other attacks in the future.

The fact was he couldn't offer her his love and promise to protect her at the same time.

Ed had been right all along. It was best to remain single. To dedicate himself to his country and his duty and forget about love. Love was not his destiny.

He might have seen off Laurent and secured Florena's future for the time being. But it had come at the cost of his heart.

'Your Majesty?'

One of his aides had come in.

'Yes?'

'You have an unexpected visitor. It isn't in your calendar but…'

Ed sighed. He wanted to go to his room. Perhaps

drown his sorrows in a few glasses of Scotch and take his frustration out on some video games. Not engage with lobbyists.

'No. Tomorrow. Or the next day. I've had enough.' He stood.

'It's Mademoiselle Auclair.'

CHAPTER TWENTY

THE LAST PERSON Simone had expected to see as she waited outside the King's offices was the Prime Minister. She'd come to say goodbye. To see Ed one final time before she flew back to Paris.

A part of her—a very large part—wanted to leave without having to go through the hurt of a proper goodbye. But he was still her friend and she owed it to him.

And he loved her.

Or thought he did.

Because Ed didn't believe in love. Or marriage. Yet last night he'd claimed to have changed his mind.

Simone didn't have an appointment. She had no right to be rocking up unannounced at his office. Thankfully one of Ed's staff—a woman who had worked in the palace for years—had recognised her and hadn't sent her away at a glance.

'Mademoiselle Auclair, it's lovely to see you. What can I do for you?'

Temporarily shocked at this formal greeting from a woman who had known her since she was a child, Simone had told her that she would like to have a few minutes with the King, if at all possible.

'He is busy at the moment, but if you can wait I will let him know you are here.' She'd smiled and motioned for Simone to sit on the large sofa in the waiting room. 'Can I get you a coffee while you wait?'

Simone had shaken her head. Her nerves were jangling enough as it was, without adding another coffee into the jittery mix.

The door to Ed's private offices opened shortly afterwards and Simone stood, expecting Ed to walk out. Instead, she came nose to nose with Pierre Laurent.

The Prime Minister froze when he saw her, and Simone saw the exact moment he recognised her. His expression hardened.

But he couldn't hurt her. Nor could his girlfriend.

She met Laurent's gaze, held it, and straightened her back. She did not need to bow to this man. She certainly didn't need to smile. This man was trying to destroy her country—not to mention Ed's life.

And your life.

She held his eyes and dared him to look away first. He couldn't hurt her. She wouldn't let him.

Laurent lowered his eyes, nodded curtly, and left the room without acknowledging anyone else.

Wow.

Endorphins rushed through her. She'd looked him in the eye and nothing had happened.

Except…not nothing. There had been a rush. Exhilaration. Victory!

The double doors opened fully and there was Ed. Wearing a bespoke suit and filling it out like…like a king. He stood with a posture that was intended to say he was ready for anything, but the paleness of his face belied his confident pose.

She wanted to run to him and pull him to her. But she'd come to say goodbye.

Hadn't she?

'Simone. Would you like to come in? Have they offered you a drink?'

'Yes—and yes.'

She stepped into the offices and the large doors were closed behind them.

She looked around, took it all in. Ed's new offices. The King's offices.

'Welcome.' Ed waved his hand around the room. 'Have you been in here before?'

She shook her head. The King's offices were not open to children. Even a prince's playmate. In the centre of the room sat a large and imposing desk. The type that would have furniture movers balking. The walls were crammed with Old Masters and portraits of Ed's ancestors.

He led her to a circle of leather armchairs, in the most comfortable-looking part of the room, and motioned for her to sit.

'Unless you'd rather go somewhere less formal?'

She shook her head. Formal was good. Formal would remind her why she'd come to say goodbye.

'I thought about doing some redecorating. But this is an official reception room and when I'm in it I am the King. Having all this around me reminds me of that.'

'Duty first,' she said.

'Not always,' he replied.

Ed met her gaze and held it. The muscles in her chest tightened. Why was this so hard?

'I just saw Laurent.'

'Ah, yes.' Ed's face brightened. 'Good news… great news, actually. He's just resigned.'

'He's what?'

'Yes—just now. I suspect he's off to announce it.'

'Wow…' She saw her recent interaction with him through a new lens. 'Why?'

'Because his girlfriend was using her PR company and various fake social media accounts to harass people. Not only you. Also members of the media. Members of the opposition. And she was doing it at his behest. He's finished.'

Simone frowned. 'I'm glad. Really glad.'

'All talk of Florena being incorporated into France should end. For the time being. I don't expect it to stop for ever. And…' He leant forward. 'I can't promise that there won't be other trolls.'

She nodded.

No wonder Laurent had scurried away when he saw her. Laurent and Morgane had been exposed and it did make her feel slightly better. But there would always be another Laurent, waiting to find a weakness in the royal family. And there would always be another Morgane waiting to humiliate one or the other of them.

But you stared him down. You looked him in the

eye and you didn't know he'd resigned. You stood in front of a powerful man, a man who had hurt you, and you didn't hide.

'Sim, why are you here?'

'I came to say…'

Goodbye.

Hadn't she?

Ed reached over and picked up her hand. He clutched it between his and her body flooded with warmth.

She never wanted to let him go.

'I meant everything I said last night. I love you, Simone,' he said. 'Not just as a friend. But as my lover, my partner, my other half. I want to spend my life with you.'

He made it sound so simple—but it wasn't.

'What if the country turns against you?

'Why would they?'

'What if they don't like me?'

'Sim, is that what you're worried about?'

'I'm worried about so many things.'

'There's only one thing you need to worry about. Only one thing we can't get through together. Do you love me?'

She opened her mouth to answer, but the words caught in her throat…behind the tears that had suddenly materialised.

She nodded. Swallowed her tears and said, 'I've always loved you. I never stopped. I tried and tried, but…'

And Ed was next to her, pulling him to her, crushing her against his chest, wiping her tears away.

'Oh, Simone… Oh, Simone… Thank goodness. We can do this. I promise. I love you so much. The people will love you when they get to know you. Besides…their King marrying his oldest friend? How can that be a bad thing?'

He was right. At least he should be. But their world would be filled with so many lies and half-truths. She'd spent fourteen years believing that she'd been sent away for embarrassing the palace, when in truth it had been for a different reason entirely. What if one of them stopped seeing the truth?

'But you're the Playboy Prince and I'm the palace crooner. What if…?'

'What if what? I don't believe any of those headlines and nor should you. You know as well as I do that they are all lies. All that matters is that you and I know what the truth is.'

He clasped her hands tighter.

'Ed, I love you,' she told him. 'With all my heart. More than anything in the world.'

It was such a relief to admit it.

He exhaled and smiled, pulling her to her feet and into his arms.

'So stay. And if the people don't like you we'll leave. I want you as my queen. But more than that I want you as my wife. I want you as my partner. Whether we're living in an attic in Paris, or in a boat on the Seine, or in a caravan in the Alps. I want you as my best friend…my soul mate.'

'Yes!' she sobbed into his chest.

'Yes to what? Living in Paris?'

'No. Yes to staying here with you.'

'Are you sure?'

'Yes. Neither of us have done anything wrong. And we will be stronger together. I've loved you all my life, and I'm not going to let what other people do or say stop us being together.'

They *were* stronger together. Together they would keep one another safe and grounded. Together they would know each other's true selves. She wouldn't be complete without him.

'Then you and I will do this together. I don't want to be apart from you for a single day.'

And he wasn't.

EPILOGUE

THE LITTLE GIRL attempted her first steps in the lush palace garden. Her father held out his hands a metre away from her mother, who gently let her go. The girl took three steps before falling into her father's arms. Both parents hugged their daughter proudly.

'It's so lovely to see children in this garden again,' said the girl's father Edouard, Duke of Armiel.

Celine, the new Duchess, kissed his cheek and steadied their daughter, Alexandria, before letting her try walking again.

'I hope that there are more children soon.' The Duke winked.

'Hang on!' Simone said. 'We'll get there one day.'

Edouard and Celine laughed.

'We've only been married a few months. Give us a chance,' Ed added.

Children would come one day, but there was no rush. Simone was getting used to one new role already: Queen of Florena.

Ed was loving having her by his side every day, but was determined she would have her own projects as well. Things that had nothing to do with her walking three steps behind him.

Her choice had been to focus on charities concerned with teenage mental health, fighting against online abuse and bullying. She had also taken a place on the board for Florena's public libraries.

Both positions into which she had thrown herself with passion and gusto.

She did still, on occasion, accompany Ed on his official duties as well. Which he loved. Because every moment she was by his side was easier and more pleasurable.

All the days.

And the nights.

Children would come in time. Children who would not be neglected or ignored. But for the time being he was enjoying having Simone to himself.

She was extremely popular everywhere they went. Any fears she'd had of being rejected by the Florenans had evaporated as soon as their relationship and then their engagement had been announced. The public had lapped up the story of two childhood friends falling in love. Furthermore, the new government had made it clear that personal and vicious abuse and threats to any member of the royal family—or indeed anyone in Florena—would not be tolerated.

Ed's father and Celine now lived in Paris, in a house much larger than Simone's attic.

Julia and André were now living in the attic, and André was running the bookshop full-time.

However, André's new landlord was a bit more relaxed than Mr Grant.

Ed had purchased the bookshop and the attic apartment for Simone as a wedding present.

She'd been horrified, but he had told her, 'I want

you to always feel that you have somewhere to run away to. I don't want you to feel trapped here.'

Simone didn't feel trapped in Florina.

She felt at home.

Queen Isabella had been back for some visits as well. In fact both the former King and Queen had attended Ed and Simone's wedding, in a feat of diplomatic gymnastics that Simone still wasn't sure how they had managed to pull off.

But they had. Because together they were much stronger than they had been apart.

The wedding had been wonderful and the press commentary all positive, although neither of them had lingered too long in following it. Their trusted aides had told them what they needed to know. Besides, after the wedding they had enjoyed a very private honeymoon in a location no one had managed to discover—Tahiti—but they kept that to themselves.

'Your son will be King Edouard the Fifth,' said Ed's father.

'No. I am the last Edouard. The fourth King.'

The curse—if there really ever had been one was lifted. By him marrying the right woman. By him making the woman he loved his queen. The kingdom would be cursed no more.

* * * * *

If you enjoyed this story,
check out these other great reads
from Justine Lewis

Back in the Greek Tycoon's World
Fiji Escape with Her Boss
Billionaire's Snowbound Marriage Reunion

All available now!